Glimpsing a photograph hadn't prepared Nick for the wrenching upheaval of meeting the boy face-to-face.

Nick cursed the fact that he'd removed his sunglasses earlier. They would have afforded at least a small measure of camouflage for the inner turbulence racking him.

Since receiving the news, he had appealed to some benevolent higher power that he'd be granted a reprieve–that a colossal mistake by an incompetent lab technician couldn't have left him with a child he hadn't known existed.

But the obvious couldn't be denied. With the force of a fist to the gut, any doubts he'd nurtured regarding the boy's paternity were instantly obliterated. He felt a recognition that couldn't be denied, an immediate and uncanny connection with this child.

This child.

His son.

Dear Reader,

Welcome to Silhouette **Special Edition**...welcome to romance. This month's six wonderful books are guaranteed to become some of your all-time favorites!

Our THAT SPECIAL WOMAN! title for March is *The Sultan's Wives* by Tracy Sinclair. An ambitious photojournalist gets herself in a predicament—the middle of a harem—when she goes in search of a hot story in an exotic land. And she finds that only the fascinating and handsome sultan can get her out of it.

This month Andrea Edwards's new series, THIS TIME, FOREVER, returns with another compelling story of predestined love in *A Rose and A Wedding Vow*. And don't miss *Baby My Baby* by Victoria Pade, as she tells the next tale of the Heller clan siblings from her series A RANCHING FAMILY.

Jake's Mountain by Christine Flynn, a spin-off to her last Special Edition title, *When Morning Comes*, rounds out the month, along with Jennifer Mikels's *Sara's Father* and *The Mother of His Child* by Ann Howard White, a new author to Special Edition.

I hope you enjoy these books, and all the stories to come!

Sincerely,

Tara Gavin
Senior Editor

Please address questions and book requests to:
Silhouette Reader Service
U.S.: 3010 Walden Ave., P.O. Box 1325, Buffalo, NY 14269
Canadian: P.O. Box 609, Fort Erie, Ont. L2A 5X3

ANN HOWARD WHITE

THE MOTHER OF HIS CHILD

Published by Silhouette Books
America's Publisher of Contemporary Romance

To Pat, Sandra and Nancy, for the weekly ritual; and Gin,
for the support.
To Anne, for knowing when to call and what to say.
And to Ed, for always.

 SILHOUETTE BOOKS

ISBN 0-373-09948-7

THE MOTHER OF HIS CHILD

Printed in U.S.A.

ANN HOWARD WHITE

discovered the romance genre straight out of three long, tedious years of law school—and instantly fell in love. She quickly became fast friends with a local bookseller who introduced her to the best the genre has to offer. Sandwiched between working with her physician/attorney husband and raising two daughters and a son, Ann read everything she could get her hands on.

She completed and sold her first book after becoming an active member of Georgia Romance Writers. She now writes full-time. The only downside, says Ann, is how much it cuts into her reading time.

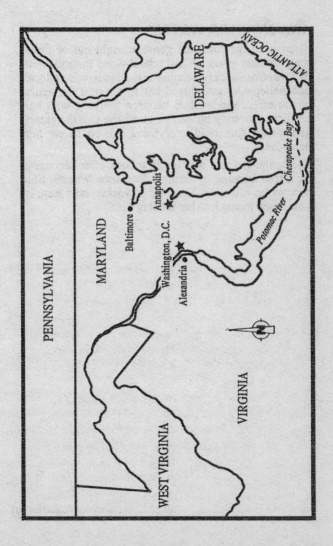

Prologue

All he had to do was open the damned file.

Nicholas Saxon fingered the edge of the color-coded manila folder with uncharacteristic indecision. Shoving the swivel chair away from the unfamiliar desk, he stood and paced to the office window. He stared grimly out at the late-afternoon skyline of the nation's capital as Ben Stanley's words echoed in his head.

I know this comes as a shock, Nick. I can't tell you how sorry I am.

Sorry? Yes, Nick was certain his old friend was sorry. Why else would Ben have left him alone in his office with a stranger's medical records? Doctors—particularly a doctor like Ben—did not intentionally leave a patient's file lying around for someone else to riffle through. Under any other circumstances, Ben's strong ethics would never allow such a scenario. But Ben and he went back a long way. They'd served together in

Vietnam. They'd been through hell and survived. And Ben felt he owed Nick.

Under any other circumstances, Ben wouldn't have informed Nick that he'd fathered a child—with a woman he'd never set eyes on!

The knowledge was still so fresh that his mind recoiled from it, denying the possibility. Nick smiled mirthlessly. *Shock* didn't begin to describe what he was feeling. He raked unsteady fingers through already rumpled hair and glanced at the innocuous-looking folder. Get it over with, Saxon. Ben wouldn't stay away forever. Purposeful strides carried Nick back to the desk. Before losing his nerve, he sat down and opened the folder in one decisive motion.

Donor Sperm Recipient: Stephanie Victoria Harcourt.

A wave of irrational resentment toward the faceless woman whose intimate statistics he now studied rolled over him. Damn it, the recipient should have been his wife; it should have been Sally, not this...this stranger. But Sally was dead. Pain and guilt, though dulled by the passage of eight years, still yawned like a cold void inside him.

Sally had asked for so little from him, from their marriage. Only a child. And he'd been unable to give her even that. His stint in Nam had taken more from him than a couple of years of his life. He'd returned home, for all practical purposes sterile. He could've lived with that. After what he'd been through, he'd had reservations about bringing a child into a world capable of inflicting the unspeakable cruelties he'd witnessed.

But Sally had been insistent that they exhaust every avenue. And according to the fertility experts they'd consulted, their one slim chance had been to stockpile his semen until a sufficient amount was collected for artificial insemination. Before Nick became completely sterile.

But before the procedure could be completed, his laughing, compassionate Sally had been snatched away. Nick had been left with emptiness and a frozen vial of potential life. In his grief, he'd instructed the clinic to destroy it. There'd never been a reason to suspect that his order hadn't been carried out.

Until Ben's call last week. Nick's wildest nightmares hadn't prepared him for a screwup like the one confronting him now.

Which brought him back to the matter of Stephanie Victoria Harcourt. Again he focused on the medical profile before him, searching for he wasn't sure what, trying to form a mental image of the woman. Her name, not to mention her address, had the ring of elite bloodlines and wealth. She'd been single, and just thirty, when she'd decided to have a child. Artificial insemination. It was such a coldly clinical, calculating way to conceive.

Why in hell had she chosen this method?

And she'd successfully delivered a child, the records confirmed. A son.

His son.

All in all, the stark data contained in the file gave little insight into the woman. One thing was clear, he thought sardonically: *he* certainly had nothing to offer a woman like her—one who'd wanted a child of her body so badly she'd resorted to artificial insemination.

Nick closed the folder with a snap, leaving it as he'd found it. His right hand tightened into a fist. As a governmental operative, he had access to the agency's most comprehensive and confidential information sources. He'd find out what he needed to know about Stephanie Harcourt. If what he'd learned today was true, this child was his flesh and blood.

The only child he would ever father.

He'd learned to be ruthless in reaching whatever goal placed before him, whether it was taking a piece of real estate in some nameless village in an equally nameless jungle, or successfully completing any one of his numerous assignments since he'd gone to work for the agency. He was accustomed to taking risks to accomplish a mission—and the cost be damned.

Somehow he'd get to his son.

Chapter One

"You want me to what?" Dr. Stephanie Harcourt asked the director of the large, privately owned, government-backed research facility that had already taken up much more of her life than she would have liked for the past four-and-a-half years.

"Take Nicholas Saxon on as your assistant," David Brown repeated. So he wouldn't have to look Stephanie in the eye, he fingered the scale model of the latest space shuttle that usually sat on one corner of his desk.

"I work alone, David. You know that." She stuffed both hands into the pockets of her pristine white lab coat, focusing her attention on her supervisor. She studiously ignored the man currently under discussion who, after a perfunctory introduction, had sauntered over to the window, carefully choosing a location just out of sight of anyone who might look in.

He propped one shoulder against the wall and folded his arms across his broad chest, almost as if preparing to be entertained. There seemed no escaping his formidable presence, she thought in irritation. It reached across the room, demanding her attention.

"I know," David said in understanding. "Hopefully it'll only be for a short time."

"This project is mine." Stephanie tried a slightly different tact. "I've given it my all," she said, a trace of anger punctuating her words. "It's taken a heck of a lot of hard work and it's almost finished. Finally. I don't want or need interference at this stage."

Assistants, Stephanie had learned, invariably slowed down rather than expedited her work. An "assistant"—also a de facto undercover government operative assigned to investigate the series of random security breaches at the lab over the last several months—was the last thing she needed.

David looked at her apologetically. "I'm afraid there's no choice."

"What do you mean, no choice?" In neat, decisive steps, Stephanie began pacing the area in front of the large desk that occupied a generous portion of the relatively small office. "My project hasn't been involved in this investigation."

"No. But it is now," he told her gently. "Someone has accessed your computer files."

Stephanie stopped pacing and stared at David in disbelief. "That's not possible," she stated flatly. "My system is protected by multiple security codes. I installed them myself. It would take more than a genius to break them."

"That may be, Dr. Harcourt." Nicholas Saxon spoke mildly from his position next to the window. "But last night someone did."

Stephanie spared a brief glance at the man still leaning against the wall before pinning her boss with a look that clearly expressed her displeasure. "Isn't this Internal Security's problem?"

"Yes." David spread his hands, as if to say he had no control over the situation. "And Security brought him in," he added, nodding toward the man across the room.

"What can he do that Security can't?"

"He's an expert with this type of investigation."

"Then he should do his job without interfering with mine." Stephanie realized she probably sounded shrewish, but at the moment she really didn't care. She didn't want this man underfoot every time she turned around. There was something almost predatory about him, something that reminded her of a jungle cat lounging in the hot sun, lounging but ready to pounce at a moment's notice.

"He's calling the shots. We've been ordered to cooperate." Below his slightly balding head, David's forehead had begun to perspire, a sure sign, Stephanie well knew, that while he might be uncomfortable with the confrontation, he wasn't going to back down. It was the same attitude she'd seen him take when he went head-to-head with Congress while defending one project or another from the budgetary ax. "We need to get to the bottom of these security breaches, Stephanie."

"I thought all this was of only minor concern."

"So far it is," David said cautiously. "But it needs to be put to rest."

"Why would anyone want to access my files?"

"That's what we'd like to know." David rose from his chair, as if the matter had been decided. "I'll leave you two alone to discuss the details," he said, heading toward the door, obviously eager to escape.

Nicholas Saxon waited until the door closed behind him before addressing Stephanie's question with one of his own. "Your project is classified, isn't it?"

She turned to face him. "Yes, but only those projects that are military in nature have been disturbed up to now. Mine isn't."

"No." He straightened away from the wall. "But it could have military application."

"You know about my work?" Stephanie asked, surprised.

"I've been briefed."

She took a moment to digest this, eyeing him as he moved toward her with lethal grace. He had a loose-limbed, unconcerned gait that spoke of extreme self-confidence. He stopped in front of her less than two feet away.

Dark brown hair containing the barest hint of gray accented a lean, hard face obviously accustomed to extensive exposure to the sun. It was a face, she decided, that looked like its owner had lived through some tough times, the harsh features intimating that he wouldn't back away from whatever was essential for survival. There was no sign of softness in him. He towered over her, dominating by his mere presence. A navy blue silk shirt encased his too-broad shoulders, enhancing the impression of carefully restrained power.

Up close he exuded a sexual energy that left her short of breath and slightly off balance. And annoyed with herself for her reactions.

But it was his eyes that had the greatest effect on her. They were almost black, and intense, concealing his own secrets while simultaneously probing for hers.

Stephanie took a half step back, then held her ground. "Apparently you weren't briefed well enough."

"Feel free to elaborate," he offered magnanimously, one side of his mouth tilting into what might be called a smile. He waited patiently, sliding his hands into the pockets of his dark slacks. The movement caused the fabric to stretch taut across his pelvis. Stephanie pulled her gaze away with a jerk.

His attitude irritated her, she reminded herself. "I don't think I can give you a physics course in the next few minutes, Mr. Saxon."

"Please," he said, not responding to the subtle insult, "call me Nick. We're going to be working together. Formal titles could seem a bit odd to the others." The hint of a smile remained, but his tone was non-negotiable. "Now tell me a little about your project. I think I can comprehend a simple overview."

"My research involves the study of black holes, supernovas, Einstein's theory of relativity." She sent him a cool look. She *wanted* to intimidate him. "In other words, the mysteries of space."

He braced himself against the edge of the desk, stretching long legs out in front of him, lazily crossing one ankle over the other. "You never know... Stephanie," he said, "who might be interested in solving mysteries."

She found his steady assessment and use of her first name unsettling. Not so much for the obvious masculine interest contained in his manner but because of some underlying question that she didn't fathom, much less want to answer. She moved a few steps farther away.

"Yes, well, whoever's been mucking around in the computers seems primarily interested in projects with a military goal. That was never the purpose of mine."

"The other guy could have different ideas." She felt his gaze following her, felt him toying with her composure. "You know, our time together will be much more pleasant if we reach an understanding."

No way in Hades, Stephanie thought heatedly, was she going to let this man come in here and take over. She'd always felt secure in her own lab. This was *her* territory. Here she was in control. Well, she conceded, in relative control anyway. Until today. And in sixty short minutes, this man had managed to destroy her sense of security.

She didn't need him taking over her timetable, jeopardizing her carefully structured, well-ordered life. She wanted, she intended, to complete her portion of this project as soon as possible.

The most important thing in her life was Jason. And he needed her now. Not that she was certain she could help him. She sighed inwardly. That was the price of having a child without benefit of a father.

Stop it, she told herself sternly. Millions of children survived being raised by one parent. She could do it. She *would* do it. Her son needed her. Nothing—certainly not this man—was going to interfere with that.

"Fine. You do your job," she said, not trying to disguise her annoyance, "and let me do mine."

Something like admiration flared in his eyes. "My job is to find out who's behind the security breaches as quickly as possible." He sauntered over to where she stood, again invading her personal space. "To do that I need your cooperation."

Stephanie drew herself up to her full height. Even at five foot eight she had to tilt her head back at an awkward angle to meet his penetrating eyes. "Why me?" she asked. "Why does it have to be my project?"

"One, it's low profile. Two, you don't have an assistant." He shrugged as if the conclusion was obvious. "It will be easier to keep my reason for being here quiet."

Stephanie folded her arms across her waist. "What kind of time frame are we looking at?"

He took in her unconsciously protective stance. "As long as it takes," he stated cryptically. "I'm afraid you're stuck with me for the duration."

And that, Stephanie decided, certainly didn't sound promising. She sighed and looked at the small, expensive watch on her left wrist. "Well, the 'duration' will have to begin on Monday."

"You have something more important to do at the moment?"

"My son, Mr. Saxon. He has a swim meet in less than an hour."

An indefinable emotion flickered in Nicholas Saxon's dark eyes. An instant later it was gone, leaving determination in its wake, tempered by a fleeting hint of vulnerability. She mentally shook her head at the contradiction. There was nothing vulnerable about this man.

"No problem," Nick said. "I'll follow you. We can talk there."

Stephanie looked at him challengingly. "I don't mix my professional life with my private one."

"In this case you don't have a choice."

This was the second time this morning that Stephanie had been told that, and she liked it less with each telling. She studied him. She'd dealt with enough males to recognize one who was used to getting what he wanted. He possessed an energy that could be considered almost threatening. But she had no intention of being manipulated. "What has my private life to do with this?"

"It seems you're a very important person."

She grimaced slightly. "Ah yes, very important—to the project. How does that affect my private life?"

"Part of my assignment," he said succinctly, "is to make sure you're safe."

Stephanie inhaled sharply, tightening her arms around her midsection to combat the shiver that feathered down her spine. "Are you suggesting that *I'm* in danger?"

"I'm not *suggesting* anything. What I'm telling you straight up is that there have been multiple security breaches at this facility. Even one places everyone here at possible risk. It's hard for me to believe that's never been pointed out to you before."

The shiver became a flutter of alarm. "Why should I trust you, Mr. Saxon?" she asked coolly, determined not to let him see the effect his words had on her.

"Do you have another choice, Dr. Harcourt?"

Good question, Stephanie thought, but the answer was self-evident. "Actually, we were warned to be careful," she admitted, a frown marring her forehead. "And to report anything suspicious." In fact, she'd had the security system at the house upgraded to state of the art shortly after the first incident. Just a logical precaution, she'd told herself.

He said nothing, yet something about his manner served to increase Stephanie's burgeoning apprehension. Because she'd always limited her projects to those of a nonmilitary nature, she'd considered herself and those around her safe.

"Is my family in danger?" He hadn't said as much. Still, the implication was there.

He made a neutral sound conveying neither confirmation nor denial.

The phone rang into the stalemate between them. Forgetting this wasn't her office, Stephanie snatched up the receiver. "Dr. Harcourt here."

"Stephie?" The sound of her sister's voice caught her by surprise. Alex seldom called her at work unless it was important. The receptionist must have transferred the call.

"Is something wrong?"

"No, no," Alex assured her. "I'm sorry to bother you, but I've got a problem with my car and need to put it in the shop. Can you pick me up at the police precinct after Jason's meet?"

"No problem. See you later." Stephanie replaced the receiver slowly, then looked at Nick Saxon. "What do you want from me?"

"Your cooperation, for starters."

"Fine, Mr. Saxon, you've got it. Anything else?"

Amusement momentarily touched his harsh features. She found the change oddly disconcerting. "Nick, remember?" he said softly.

She inclined her head slightly in a gesture of acquiescence, but she didn't put word to action. "And?"

"As much information as you have as fast as you can give it to me."

"You don't ask for much, do you?"

There was the briefest hesitation, and a muscle flexed at his jaw. "Only what's necessary."

"Do you dislike people in general or just me in particular?"

"I don't like or dislike you, Dr. Harcourt. You're simply an obstacle I have to deal with."

Well, that certainly put her in her place. A new thought struck her. "You're not going to be underfoot round the clock, are you?" she asked, remembering that some scientists at the lab had been assigned bodyguards as a precautionary measure because of the sensitive nature of their work.

Instead of answering, he smiled that smile again— little more than a movement of his lips. But she could understand, she thought grudgingly, how some women might find it sexy. He checked his watch. It was large and black, the kind divers wore. "Don't we have a swim meet to get to?" he reminded her, an odd urgency entering his voice.

Stephanie chafed under his authoritative manner. She might as well concede defeat gracefully, she told herself. The sooner Nicholas Saxon got what he wanted, the sooner she would be rid of him.

"Do you have children . . . Nick?"

His head came up and she was pinned by the undiluted impact of his dark eyes. "At the moment no one calls me Dad."

That meant he probably had no idea how long and hot and very tiring an amateur swim meet could be, Stephanie thought almost gleefully. "All right. Let me get my things."

She led the way to her office and left Nick to investigate his surroundings on his own, leaving her free to close down the lab. He wandered over to her desk, idly picking up a picture of Jason. It was a photograph taken of him standing beside her telescope at home, grinning. Nick studied the picture for long moments, an unreadable expression on his face.

This was not shaping up to be a good day, Stephanie decided. First this man was shoved under her nose at work. Now he was going to intrude in her private life. He was pushy as hell, she silently fumed—not just surface pushy, but deep-down pushy. And don't forget irritating, she reminded herself.

Bottom line was that she wanted him out of her lab and out of her life. The man stirred feelings in her she knew were best left alone. There was a determination about him that was subtle, yet compelling. Something told her that trusting Nick Saxon was only for the foolhardy.

"Ready?" she finally asked.

"Yeah," he said, gently replacing the photograph.

"Well, come on then." She waited for him to precede her out the door. "I think you're in for a surprise."

A surprise. That pretty much summed up his present situation.

Eyes narrowed, Nick studied the graceful movements of the woman ahead of him as she quickly walked toward her car, parked in the reserved section just outside the building that housed her laboratory. Analyzing Stephanie helped him control the emotions that chewed at him every time he thought about where they were headed.

There was a natural elegance about her that had seemed out of place in the sterile surroundings of the lab. He'd noticed it the moment he'd first seen her, only seconds before her model-perfect figure had caught his attention. Even under her starched lab coat he'd been able to tell she was willowy, but not lacking the right amount of padding in all the right places.

Her medium-length hair was a warm shade of light brown. And thick. The kind of hair that made a man want to discover if his hands could tame it.

She'd discarded the coat before leaving the building. Under it she wore slacks and a soft pink, gauzy shirt that looked comfortable in the July heat. She was somewhere around five-eight, he estimated, with most of her height taken up by long legs.

Against his will, he felt a tightening in his groin. Hell. He needed to keep his mind above his waist. Hormones, he told himself. How long had it been since he'd last been out with a woman?

He could see how some men might find this woman attractive, he admitted with detached interest. But not him. His goal was to get acquainted with his son.

Stephanie Victoria Harcourt might not be what he'd expected, but he knew the rules. If he wanted to succeed, he had to remain objective.

Nick followed her silver Mercedes out of the compound at a discreet distance—close enough to keep Stephanie in view but far enough away so that he wouldn't spook her. With a twinge of conscience, he remembered the momentary glimmer of fear he'd put in her tawny green eyes. But he ruthlessly suppressed it. He couldn't afford to feel sympathy for her, he reminded himself. Or guilt. He couldn't afford to second-guess himself. She was key to something he wanted, something too vital, too precious to him personally to permit even a moment's weakness.

Learning he was a father had forced him to reevaluate everything he'd come to believe in since his wife's death. For self-preservation, he'd cloaked himself in animosity toward the woman who'd usurped the position that should have been Sally's. All he wanted, all he intended, was to establish a link, a bond, with his son. But now that he'd met Stephanie Harcourt...

He shook off the thought before it was fully formed. In his line of work, Nick had learned to be ruthless when dealing with a potential adversary. And the woman *was* his adversary. To forget that cold, hard truth could cost him dearly.

He'd do what had to be done to accomplish his mission.

He'd done his homework on Dr. Stephanie Harcourt—or had tried. What he'd found was that she was elusive and exceptionally well protected for an average citizen. Data on her was hard to come by. He knew she was thirty-eight, that she'd attended some of the most exclusive schools in the nation, that she rarely if ever dated and had little or no social life apart from a sister. And that she'd chosen to have a baby by artificial insemination. He knew a great deal about her—and nothing at all.

What kind of mother was she? What kind of relationship did she have with his son? Was Jason happy? She'd made it crystal clear earlier today, Nick recalled, just how involved her project was and just how vital it was to her to get it completed. How important could a child be to a mother so dedicated to such a demanding profession?

He had to give her credit. She was almost as good at concealing what was going on in her head as he was. Almost. If there was any other way of getting to his son without dealing with the kid's mother, Nick would have taken it. But dealing with Stephanie Harcourt was absolutely necessary—he'd conceded that.

He rubbed the back of his neck, trying to ease the tension. He had his work cut out for him.

The century-old country club where the swim meet was being held was located just outside D.C. in one of the more prestigious sections of Maryland. The wait for Jason seemed interminable, and to fill the time, Nick asked Stephanie routine questions about her work— questions he'd used as the excuse for tagging along with her in the first place.

It wasn't until the first break, as they were heading for the clubhouse, that Jason hailed his mother from the other side of the pool apron and headed in their direction. "Hey, Mom!"

Stephanie stopped and waved.

Nick braced himself emotionally as Jason caught up with them. Glimpsing his child in a photograph or from a distance hadn't prepared him for the wrenching upheaval of meeting him face-to-face. He cursed the fact that he'd removed his dark glasses earlier. They would have afforded at least a small measure of camouflage for the inner turbulence racking him.

Over the weeks since receiving the staggering news from Ben, Nick had appealed to some benevolent higher power that he'd be granted a reprieve—that a colossal screwup by an incompetent lab technician couldn't have left him with a child he hadn't known existed for seven years. But the obvious couldn't be denied. With the force of a fist to the gut, any doubts he'd nurtured regarding the boy's paternity were instantly obliterated. He felt an immediate and uncanny connection with this child. A recognition that couldn't be denied. It left him shaken to the core.

His son.

"Jason," Stephanie said, "this is Mr. Saxon. He'll be working with me at the lab for a while." She smiled down at the boy. "Nick, this is my son, Jason."

The boy was tall for his age, with serious dark eyes that studied Nick with an intelligent interest beyond his seven-plus years. The urge to enfold his son in a massive bear hug was as disturbing to Nick as it was overwhelming. And difficult to contain. He extended his hand. "Nice to meet you, Jason."

Jason politely shook the man's hand. "Hi, Mr. Saxon."

"Please call me Nick. I have a couple of nieces and nephews about your age. That's what they call me." But it wasn't what he wanted his son to call him. "You're a pretty good swimmer."

"Thanks," Jason said, but dejection shadowed his face. "I'm okay, I guess."

"You guess?" Nick wanted to put his hand on Jason's shoulder or ruffle his hair, but realized either gesture, particularly from a stranger, might make the seven-year-old uncomfortable. The thought hurt. He slid his hands into his pockets and nodded his understanding of the competitive male spirit. "You came in first in two events."

"Yeah, but my times sucked."

"Jason," Stephanie reprimanded affectionately, brushing a lock of soggy, tawny brown hair out of her son's eyes and adjusting the neon-colored towel more snugly around his thin shoulders.

The boy tolerated her ministrations with long-suffering patience and gave her a sheepish smile. "Sorry, Mom."

The easy affection between mother and son was immediately apparent to Nick. He struggled against the shaft of pure envy that ripped through him. It angered him that, through no fault of his own, he didn't have the right to touch his son in the same casual manner.

The range of emotions besieging Nick was almost more than he could handle. He thought he'd come to terms with his sterility—with the fact that he'd never be a father.

But that was before discovering he already had a child.

"Aren't you being a little rough on yourself?" he said, tamping down the turbulent thoughts. "You did a super job for your team. That counts for something, doesn't it?"

"I guess. But if my times don't improve, I won't keep coming in first."

"You know, sometimes coming in first isn't the most important thing in life."

Jason looked doubtful. "Yeah, well, it is if the team's depending on you."

"Did your coach tell you that?" Nick asked. He was well acquainted with the drive to achieve, but wondered why a kid Jason's age would seem so concerned with winning.

"Nah." Jason shrugged, causing his towel to slide again down one shoulder. "He just says I should keep working on my arm motion in backstroke and my turns in the medley." Even in the heat of the early-afternoon sun, he shivered slightly and tugged the contrary towel back into place. "I could probably cut a few tenths of a second off my times if I could do them smoother."

Nick found himself hungrily searching for traces of himself in the boy. He remembered being a gangly kid, all arms and legs, but with more than his share of raw determination. Nick noted with unfamiliar paternal pride that Jason was like himself at that age, distinct advantages for a swimmer. Combined with his competitive nature, Jason would do all right in the long run.

He was bright and mature, Nick thought, but a kid his age shouldn't be worrying about tenths of seconds. He should be enjoying the friendly competition and camaraderie with his teammates. Of course, Nick had to admit, he'd always had that same drive. It wasn't necessarily a trait he wanted to pass on to a child. *His son.* The stark reality of it still had the power to knock the breath out of him.

Damn it, he wanted the right to ask about every aspect of Jason's life, about all the routine things that had happened to him—things that most fathers knew about their children from the day they were born.

Stephanie shifted and he glanced at her, noting the slight frown marring her smooth forehead. She'd been quiet throughout the exchange between them. Apparently something bothered her, too. Did she understand the problems that troubled a boy? Was she even interested? He'd make it his business to find out.

"Tell you what. I'm a fair swimmer, and I might be able to give you a few pointers." Nick sensed Stephanie stiffen beside him. "That is, if your mom doesn't object."

Jason looked at him with youthful skepticism. "Were you ever on a swim team?"

Nick grinned. "Not like yours. But I had a pretty good teacher."

"Yeah? Who?"

"Do the Navy SEALs count?"

"Wow! Really?" Jason brightened immediately. "I read about them in school. Were you one for a long time?"

The hellish images of his final months of service flashed through Nick's mind. *A damned sight longer than was healthy.* "Long enough to learn a few tricks about swimming."

"And you could teach me? That'd be great!" Jason said, his enthusiasm growing by the second. "Wouldn't it, Mom?"

"Well," Stephanie hedged.

"When could we start?" Jason asked, plowing on. "Could you—"

"Hey, Harcourt! C'mon," someone yelled as a group of swimmers burst through the large glass doors fronting the clubhouse.

Jason turned and waved to his teammates, then faced Nick again. "I gotta go. It's our turn to warm up."

"Harcourt, you coming?" a voice called again, this time more impatiently.

Not Harcourt, a part of Nick raged. *Your name should be Saxon.* He wondered fleetingly what name appeared under Father on Jason's birth certificate. Or had it been left blank—a fitting symbol of the place he held in his son's life?

"Coming." Jason looked expectantly at Nick. "Will you be here after we finish?"

"Jason..." Stephanie began.

"I'm not going anywhere," Nick told him quietly. He stuffed his hands deeper into the pockets of his slacks to keep from reaching out to his son—and to ease the sudden ache in his chest.

To Stephanie his words sounded more than a promise.

Chapter Two

Nick's gaze followed Jason hungrily until he caught up with his friends. "He's a great kid."

"Thank you. I think so." Sensing the coiled tension in him, Stephanie glanced questioningly at the man beside her. Outwardly he appeared relaxed. But it was the quiet intensity with which he studied the scene before him, as if he couldn't afford to miss a single detail, that belied his relaxed stance and left her feeling as though there was something more going on than met the eye.

She cleared her throat. "And thank you for the advice you gave him about swimming." That Nick had reiterated the same arguments she'd used repeatedly with Jason surprised her. Here was a male ally who shared her own sentiments about competition. What other areas of raising a boy would they agree on? she wondered fleetingly. "I've been trying to tell him to lighten up on himself for some time."

"My pleasure." As Jason was absorbed into the swarm of teammates, Nick returned his attention to her. "I meant what I said. I'd be happy to give him some pointers."

Something about the empathetic interest Nick had shown Jason was at odds with the no-nonsense demeanor she'd witnessed earlier at the lab. She had the curious sensation that this man was crowding her. That, added to her nagging concern about her own ability to deal with her son's problems, made her defensive. "Thanks, but I don't think that would be such a good idea. As I said earlier, I don't mix my professional and private lives."

"I think I'm being dismissed." He grinned, but something hard-edged flared in his eyes, to be extinguished so quickly Stephanie questioned whether she'd witnessed it.

"Why do you assume someone isn't already working with him?" she asked impulsively.

His probing gaze sharpened. "Is there?" he queried. "A husband, maybe?" His voice roughened. "His father?"

At best it was an impertinent question; at worst it was none of his business. But some unnamed emotion he seemed to hold tightly checked prompted Stephanie to answer. "No husband. No—" she exhaled a quick breath "—father. Just his coach."

A slight frown wrinkled her forehead. Nick sensed he was pushing too hard. She was skittish as it was. If he wasn't careful, he was going to make her suspicious. "Can I get you a cold drink?" he asked, to slow the steadily building tension.

Stephanie glanced at her watch, then out at the team swimming warm-up laps in the pool. They had a few minutes before the second half began. "That would be nice."

Nick guided her through the thinning crowd inside the clubhouse, over to the polished-oak bar, and ordered two soft drinks. After taking a couple of swallows, he said casually, "Jason just needs a boost to his self-confidence."

"Why all the interest in my son, Mr. Saxon?"

"I see we're back to formal titles."

"In this town, I believe that's called evading the question."

"Are you into politics, Dr. Harcourt?" he countered.

She took a sip of her cola and considered his question. "Not in the usual meaning of the word."

One side of his mouth quirked. "It seems we can both be evasive."

"Then you're admitting you're evasive?" she asked mildly.

Resentment surged through him, demanding an outlet. On some objective level he recognized that what he felt was unreasonable; she was no more to blame for this mess than he was. But that didn't diminish the stakes. Hell, how did that adage go? The best defense was a good offense.

"Do you challenge everyone who shows an interest in Jason?"

"If he's a total stranger, yes." She slanted him a censuring look. "It's a dangerous world, Mr. Saxon."

Touché, he silently applauded. On the one hand he had to appreciate her protective instincts where his son was concerned. On the other it frustrated him that slipping past her guard was going to be trickier than he'd anticipated.

"True, you can never be too cautious," he commented.

"I'm so relieved you agree."

Nick chuckled at the faint hint of sarcasm and felt an unexpected sexual jolt. Her spunk had a disturbingly seductive effect on him. "But then you already know my credentials."

Stephanie watched, fascinated, as his eyes warmed, tiny crinkles appearing at the corners. The disarming grin sent a frisson of excitement scurrying through her, making her feel oddly exposed. "Yes, and as I recall they don't include interfering in my son's life."

"Maybe. But since I'm going to be a part of your life—and his—for a while, I thought I might offer some harmless advice."

She'd learned over the years to trust her intuition about people—especially men. No way could this man ever be considered harmless. Something about him tempted, yet frightened, her. The contradiction of determination and vulnerability she sensed in him was potent. It wasn't a combination with which she felt comfortable. "I think it best if we keep this relationship on a professional footing."

Nick concentrated on his plastic cup for several seconds, as if some answer might be found within the dregs of the soft drink. "You think so?"

She looked startled. "What do you mean?"

"We're going to be living in each other's pockets. We'll get to know a lot about each other."

"What's that got to do with giving me advice on how to raise my son?"

"You don't seem to be a person who'd pass up an opportunity to learn something that could be useful," he said, injecting a lighter note into his voice.

"And you think you have something useful to offer?" Stephanie drawled.

He ignored the jab. "If I'm to protect you, I need to learn all I can about you. And you need to learn about me."

"Why would I want to know anything about you?"

Downing the last few swallows of his drink, Nick crushed the empty container in one strong fist and threw it into a nearby trash can. "You need to trust me."

Stephanie studied him for several heartbeats. She thought she'd been manipulated by the best, but this man was a master. "Why?"

Nick returned her unblinking gaze. "In the long run, it could save you a great deal of grief."

"All right." She exhaled sharply and crossed her arms. "What is it you think I should know?"

"Let's start with the basics," he said. "I own a small farm just outside Alexandria, Virginia."

A farm? Not what Stephanie would have expected from this man. She mentally shook herself. She did not want to know about his personal life. "I'm not—"

"I'm in excellent health and have no communicable diseases."

"You don't—"

"I'm single. And," he added, "at the moment I have no romantic attachments."

Why did that bit of information cause her heart to miss a beat? Stephanie wondered in irritation. "This really isn't necessary, Nick."

"Ah, but I think it is, Stephanie."

She wasn't oblivious to a subtle vehemence that underlay his teasing.

He leaned against the bar, forcing rigid muscles to relax. "How else am I going to convince you that I'm not a menace?"

"Why do you find it necessary to convince me of anything?"

"To protect my reputation?" Again he grinned. "I come from a large family," he continued. "Four brothers, two sisters, lots of nieces and nephews. That's why I have an idea what's troubling Jason."

That got her attention. "Oh?"

"He's hung up on winning," he said evenly. "And that concerns you." He cocked a dark eyebrow. "Am I right?"

She'd bet the family art collection that this man was a formidable foe when facing an enemy—or any opponent, for that matter. His intuition was astonishing, considering that most parents wanted their children to excel, sometimes going to outrageous lengths to encourage them. "Partially," she hedged. "My primary concern is that he's too hard on himself."

Nick's tension eased marginally. "In what way?"

Stephanie debated whether she should discuss this with a stranger. But then again, what could it hurt? For whatever reason, Nick seemed interested. He'd given good advice earlier. What harm was there in getting a male opinion?

"He never seems to please himself. He's always striving to do—" Stephanie gestured erratically "—whatever, just a little bit better." An expression of frustrated concern marred her features. "Why can't he be happy with his successes?"

The genuine distress in Stephanie's question touched Nick in ways he hadn't expected. And certainly didn't want. But it didn't stop him from offering reassurance.

"Taking care of a child alone in today's world isn't easy. Raising a son is even tougher."

She looked at him, again surprised at his perception. "How would you know?"

He lifted one powerful shoulder. "Large family, remember? Most kids, especially boys, have a competitive nature. It's not unusual."

"Yes, but he doesn't take time to enjoy what he's already done. Is it normal for a seven-year-old to have a driving need to always surpass his latest accomplishment?"

But a part of Stephanie knew the answer, understood what drove her son—and that's what made her ache. She'd lived it herself—trying to please her peers, to escape their cruel taunts, to make up for the fact that she was different. Oh yes, she understood what her son was doing and why he was doing it. And it was breaking her heart.

She'd hoped Jason would escape that burden. She'd wanted an ordinary, uncomplicated childhood for him. As different from her own as she could make it.

"Sometimes kids act this way to get attention," Nick said quietly.

Stephanie heard the unspoken inquiry in the mild comment and it added to her guilt. How many times had she asked herself if she was spending enough time with Jason? If she was providing him with the support he needed? If she was somehow at fault for his dissatisfaction with himself?

Most of all, if she had selfishly cheated him of a father?

This wasn't like her. She was an extremely private person, had learned to be because of her unusual upbringing. And she *always* shielded Jason from exposure to strangers. Yet, in a matter of minutes, she'd just told this man more about her son than she'd ever told anyone.

Feeling confused and strangely vulnerable, she glanced at her watch. "We should get back outside," she said. "The referee will be calling the second half any minute now."

Her withdrawal didn't bother Nick. He'd planted the seed. Now he'd let her have some space. Just enough so she didn't feel too threatened.

He could be patient. For a while.

How she'd come to be entering the Burger Barn two hours later with Nick Saxon, Stephanie wasn't certain. Her son had a devious streak in him, she decided in good-natured exasperation. Just like his Aunt Alex. An exuberant Jason had taken it upon himself to invite Nick to join them in the victory celebration after the meet. And it was too much to hope that the man would decline—even after Stephanie had made a point of telling him what a madhouse he'd be forced to endure.

Sighing inwardly, she surveyed the line that snaked through the busy fast-food house. The mouth-watering smells of grilled hamburgers and french fries didn't tempt her appetite as they usually did. She sent up a small prayer of thanks for the mass of soggy kids and assorted parents that gave her a sense of insulation, albeit false, from the man a half step behind her in line. He seemed to have an uncanny knack for subtly provoking her. She didn't want to examine too closely why that should be.

"Is it always this crowded?" Nick asked scant millimeters from Stephanie's ear, so that she could hear him over the din.

The intimate feel of his warm breath on the nape of her neck startled her. "After a meet?" She discreetly placed several inches between them and sent him a half smile over her shoulder, hoping he couldn't hear the rapid tattoo of her heart against her ribs. "Always."

"Yeah," Jason chimed in, his face beaming. "Isn't it great?"

"Not exactly my choice of words," Nick muttered, his tone rueful.

"You don't like crowds," Stephanie observed.

"No."

"I warned you," she reminded him sweetly as a group of excited kids pushed their way through the line, almost knocking her off balance. Nick automatically reached out to steady her. His strong hand on her upper arm sent a jolt of awareness through her. She pulled against his grip.

For a heartbeat he didn't release her, his fingers burning an indelible impression into her skin—and her senses. Then his hand was gone and she was free.

"So you did." He collected their orders and looked around for a place to sit in the room overflowing with kids and adults. "There's a table in the corner."

Jason bounced from one foot to the other trying to peer through the wall of people. "Hurry, Mom, Nick, follow me," he yelled, darting ahead of them, clutching the ever-present backpack containing his boyish treasures in a death grip.

"Hey, he's pretty good," Nick said as they followed in his wake, elbowing and jostling their way toward the vacant booth.

"He's had lots of practice." Stephanie slid onto the bench and began divvying up the food.

Jason grabbed a hamburger and settled beside Nick. "It's really neat that you're going to help me with my swimming."

"Neat, huh?" One side of Nick's mouth kicked up into a smile. It softened his features, making him appear less...*dangerous*. Stephanie didn't like what that observation did to her pulse rate.

"Yeah. The guys think it's great. And I can sure use it, too." Jason took a large bite of his hamburger.

Stephanie raised one eyebrow and sent her son a reproving look. "To hear you talk, one would never guess you already swim like a fish."

"You don't understand, Mom. This is guy stuff."

Her son's offhand remark hurt. Stephanie picked up a french fry and nibbled at it, primarily to give her something to do. No, she didn't understand. She wasn't even sure what "guy stuff" was. She was certain she didn't know how to deal with it.

Recently she'd had to admit that Jason needed a male influence in his life. She could provide for most of his needs, but not the essential interaction and bonding a boy needed with a man. It was something she hadn't realized could be a problem when she'd made the difficult decision to have a child eight years ago. But she'd find a way to deal with it, she assured herself. Jason was the most precious thing in her life, made more so by what she'd had to go through to have him.

"Mom's great," Jason said to Nick in a confidential whisper, "but she's not very helpful with swimming."

"Oh? And girls don't know about swimming?" she asked teasingly, forcing the troubling thoughts away.

Jason looked a little sheepish. "Mom...!" he said in exasperation, then turned to Nick for support. "Tell her girls can't know about guy stuff."

Something flickered in the man's hard features, to be quickly replaced by a grin that Stephanie wasn't certain was entirely genuine. "Maybe not. But she's pretty good at other things. Right?"

Instinct told Stephanie that it was more than a rhetorical question, and she found herself holding her breath, awaiting her son's answer.

"Well, yeah." Jason looked at his mother as if gauging her value. "She's great at explaining science and stuff. Did you know that the closest star is Alpha Centauri and it's 4.3 light-years away? That's about twenty-five trillion..." His words suddenly trailed off. "Anyway, it's really far."

"Sounds interesting," Nick commented, encouraging him to continue.

"Yeah," Jason said, but his earlier enthusiasm was missing. "But Mom doesn't know about real important things," he repeated.

"I see," Nick said, and took a bite of cheeseburger.

And that summed up her worth to her son, Stephanie thought with a pang. At least she knew Jason had learned, if not always enjoyed, what she'd tried to teach him about her work. "Thanks for the recommendation, young man."

"Oh, Mom," Jason said, dismissing his mother's remark with an apologetic grin. "Of course, she's real busy at work," he said, trying to defend her to Nick. "So she doesn't have a lot of time." He chewed on a french fry. "So when can we start?"

"Maybe Nick has other things he has to do," Stephanie suggested mildly, looking directly at him. Not every man would tolerate working with a child who wasn't his own, particularly if he had no children himself. So Nick's interest in Jason was probably temporary at best.

Nick's dark eyes held hers for a beat. "If that were the case, I wouldn't have offered." He returned his attention to Jason. "Looks like we'll have to work it out with your mom first."

It was a challenge. Stephanie's carefully cultivated intuition whispered caution. He did seem genuinely interested in what Jason was saying, which surprised her. Few men were willing to pay attention to the prattle of a seven-year-old, even if the child was just below the genius level. But her natural suspicion asked why this man should be different. What was he really after? She didn't want Jason getting his hopes up, only to have them crushed.

Jason looked expectantly at Stephanie. "Mom?"

"You're the volunteer," she said to Nick, lobbing the ball back into his court. "What's your suggestion?"

He pushed aside his half-eaten burger. "How does a couple of sessions a week sound?"

"Aw right!" Jason exclaimed. "Can we start this week?"

"Is the club available?" Nick asked Stephanie, picking up a Rubik's Cube from among the things Jason had dumped on the table as soon as they sat down.

She nodded. "Of course, it's extremely crowded," she said with some relish, watching him turn the multicolored, four-inch-cube puzzle over and over in his hand. Absently he began trying to align the matching colors.

"Yeah, there's so many people, there's no room to swim," Jason added, just to make certain no one missed the point.

After several attempts, Nick put the cube down. "Crowded," he said, then grimaced. Crowds made him feel trapped, uneasy. He'd learned to prefer open spaces, where he had a better chance of spotting potential dangers. "You don't happen to have a pool in your backyard, do you?"

Jason heaved a regretful sigh. "No, but I sure wish we did."

An image of the architecturally flawless, professionally decorated masterpiece where she, Jason and Alex resided came to Stephanie's mind. The house had been perfect for the many extravagant parties her parents had held regularly for members of the diplomatic social set. Her mother had considered a swimming pool unacceptable amidst the imposing decor, although more than one guest had ended up swimming with the goldfish in the reflecting pool on the back grounds. Stephanie smiled wryly.

Nick shrugged. "Well, there's always Plan B."

"Plan B?" Stephanie asked.

"My pool."

"Your own private pool?"

He nodded and grinned. "Don't sound so shocked. Lots of people have them."

"Hey, a pool. That's neat," Jason said.

Secluded in a private pool...with this man? That definitely wasn't Stephanie's idea of neat.

"You're welcome to use mine anytime your mom will let you."

Jason cast a quick glance at his mother, sizing up his chances of success if he pushed the issue.

"Jason, why don't you go find your friends until we're ready to leave?" Stephanie suggested.

The boy rolled his eyes, then looked at Nick. "That means she's going to talk about something she doesn't want me to hear. Moms think kids are so dumb." He slid off the bench. "Don't let her change your mind, okay?"

"Don't worry." Nick sent him a lopsided grin. "It would take an awful lot to do that."

Her son's parting appeal to Nick set up a sharp ache inside Stephanie. "Don't be gone too long," she cautioned Jason. "We have to pick up Alex."

"Okay, Mom. See you later, Nick." Grabbing the rest of his soft drink and his backpack of treasures, he trudged off into the milling crowd.

Uneasiness stirred in Nick. Who, and how important, was this Alex? He knew Stephanie had no husband, but he'd somehow overlooked the possibility of there being another man on the scene. Frustration momentarily masked his unease. Hell, she was attractive—and, he grudgingly admitted, *sexy*—enough to have dozens of men sniffing around. Damn it, he was used to asking direct questions to get answers. But he was aware she had a suspicious nature. He knew he had to tread softly with this woman, and treading softly wasn't his strong suit.

Time. What he needed was time. And patience. In a few short weeks his whole world had been turned upside down, his goals and perspective on life shifting 180 degrees. A sense of urgency squeezed his chest. How much time did he have to accomplish his objective? And what exactly *was* his objective, he wondered, now that the doubts he'd clung to regarding Jason's paternity had been wiped out?

"You're making an awful lot of promises to him," Stephanie said as soon as her son was out of earshot. She was suddenly aware that the very crowd that earlier had given her a sense of insulation from Nick Saxon now seemed to isolate them in their own private world.

She retrieved the Rubik's Cube, which Jason had left behind. Within seconds she'd squared all the colors, disassembled it and repeated the process.

"I don't think I've ever met anyone who could work that puzzle," he remarked, disregarding her comment. "In fact, I'd begun to think it wasn't possible."

She glanced up to find him watching her steadily. Something fluttered low in her stomach. When he studied her like this, which seemed far too often for her peace of mind, she felt as though he could read each of her secrets. Inwardly she shook her head. Lord, her wariness was getting out of hand.

"Once you learn how to solve it," she said, striving for nonchalance, "it's not hard."

"Hey, don't be modest. I'm impressed." Nick studied her flushed cheeks and was surprised by the odd impulse to reach over and stroke their warmth. "Maybe you could give me some tips. That thing has always made me feel a little less than bright."

Stephanie set the game aside. "I can't imagine you feeling inferior to much of anything."

"Everyone feels inferior at one time or another." A muscle jumped in his jaw. "We seem to have gotten away from the original topic of swimming."

The man was a master at manipulating the conversation, Stephanie observed, not for the first time. Obviously there were areas of his own personal life that he wasn't any more eager to discuss than she was hers. "What about your assignment?"

"I don't work all the time. I do take an occasional break." It wasn't a complete lie, Nick told himself, but then admitted that it was. He'd submerged himself in work since Sally's death, taking on far more dangerous assignments than was healthy. He hadn't wanted any free time—time in which all the bittersweet memories could torment him.

But now things had changed dramatically for Nick. And because of that, his partner was somewhere out there on his own in a potentially dangerous situation.

"And you don't have anything better to do with your spare time than spend it with strangers?"

"Are you always this suspicious?" he countered.

"Always. A lesson I learned very early in life is to look all gift horses in the mouth. There's always an angle. I'm just wondering what yours is."

"Look at it this way," Nick said, ignoring her implied question and his conscience. "Swimming might be the distraction we need to make this assignment less awkward for all of us."

That made sense. She *was* overreacting. The man was simply doing his job. And showing an interest in her son in the bargain. Jason certainly appeared appreciative of the attention. "You seem to have everything all worked out." She didn't have control of this situation, and she was finding that fact extremely unnerving. "Unfortunately, we seem to be stuck with you for the present. But I won't have Jason hurt under any circumstances. Be careful what you promise him. He may appear to be a self-assured little boy, but he can be wounded very easily."

Nick returned her direct stare. "Something you should remember about me," he stated in a precise tone, "is that I never say what I don't mean."

She assessed the sincerity in his eyes. What she found there made her feel only marginally better.

Nick looked at his watch. "You think about it," he said as he got to his feet. He rapped a knuckle on the table, an audible signal that their conversation was ended. "Either way, I'll be in touch."

It sounded like a vow.

Chapter Three

"Sounds like the man's a hunk," Alex said as Stephanie drove the silver Mercedes through an electronic gate in the security fence surrounding their private property. "Not to mention sexy as hell."

Stephanie glanced in the rearview mirror to make sure Jason was still busy reading. He'd had his nose in that book ever since they'd left Nick and gone to pick up Alex. "I don't believe those were my exact words," she commented dryly, wondering just what it was she'd said that would lead her younger sister to draw those conclusions.

"Please," Alex said, waving one perfectly manicured hand for emphasis, "I'm reading between the lines here."

Under her breath, Stephanie counted to twenty in several foreign languages, then in English for good measure. She proceeded down the long curving driveway, finally stopping in front of the spacious, ultra modern residence. Set well back on heavily wooded grounds, the house couldn't be seen from the main road.

"Well, that certainly explains it then. I swear, Alex, your fantasies are better than any I could ever dream up." She set the emergency brake with deliberate precision and opened the car door. "Come to think of it, he's just your type."

"Oh?" Alex asked with interest. "And just what is my type?"

"A man who needs his ego deflated," Stephanie muttered. "Don't forget to bring your things," she reminded her son as he clambered from the car.

"Hmm." Alex glanced at her sister. "I guess that means you're not going to give him a chance."

"For goodness' sake, the man's part of lab security."

"Sure." Alex followed Stephanie and Jason up the circular steps that led to an elaborate front door fashioned with intricate geometric patterns in stained glass. "It sure sounds as though he doesn't have anything better to do with his free time than give lessons to a seven-year-old who already swims like Mark Spitz. Obviously he doesn't have the slightest interest in the kid's mother."

Stephanie concentrated on inserting her key into the lock and opening the door. "He's interested in something, all right," she said under her breath as she disengaged the alarm system. "But it's not me."

"Okay, then explain it to me. Why else would he want to hang around when he's off duty?" Alex persisted.

Stephanie had wondered the same thing herself. How had she, in the space of eight short hours, wound up

saddled with a man who radiated more than a hint of
danger and who was not only playing havoc with her
professional life but her personal life as well? She entered the huge, airy entrance hall that provided an impressive view of the grand living room a half flight
below.

"Probably just to aggravate me." The man was certainly arrogant enough. Stephanie kicked off her shoes
and ran lightly down the steps to the stereo system hidden in a massive entertainment center. She needed
something to soothe her frazzled nerves. "Jason, go up
and change your clothes," she said to her son, who'd
trudged in behind her, still absorbed in his book. "And
don't forget to hang up your wet things to dry."

"'Kay, Mom," he said absently, heading up the
stairs.

Alex flopped down on one of the stark, black leather
sofas, propping her long legs on the enormous glass
coffee table, and watched her sister through narrowed
eyes. "You simply won't consider that a man might be
interested in you."

"No. I'm just being realistic. Past experience is a
great teacher." She selected several CDs, including a
range of soft pieces from classical to country, and inserted them into the disk player. The music wrapped
around her, welcoming and warming. It seemed to give
the rather sterile house a modicum of personality.

"There speaks the scientist," Alex chided gently.

"You're not going to let this drop, are you?"

Her younger sister lifted one shoulder and smiled
wickedly.

"What do you suggest I do?" Stephanie asked archly.
"Kidnap the poor man and force him to do my bid-
ding?"

"Ah, then you admit your thoughts about him have been more than merely platonic?"

Her sister's teasing generated a disturbing flutter deep within Stephanie. "May I remind you that not everyone has your knack for deluding men into believing whatever you want?" On more than one occasion Stephanie had watched, fascinated, as Alex convinced a man that the world was flat, or that she was a dumb blonde. It was an ability Stephanie envied. Not that she personally wanted to be blond—she was content with her own tawny brown hair. But the "dumb" element of that equation was singularly appealing. In fact, she'd settle for simply "average." That any grown man could be intimidated by an intelligent female never ceased to amaze her.

In her experience, people in general and men in particular had a hidden agenda—and it usually had something to do with the use of her brains. She conceded that her experience was limited to primarily professional situations, but she'd learned enough to be wary.

"I'll be happy to teach you all my tricks," Alex offered magnanimously.

Stephanie rolled her eyes and suppressed a smile. At times Alex could be downright incorrigible. She pushed a button to channel the music to her suite on the upper floor. "I'm going to shower," she said, following Jason's earlier route up the wide, curving staircase that was more aesthetic than utilitarian.

"Chicken," Alex muttered to Stephanie's retreating back.

She ignored the remark. At the moment she felt too vulnerable to deal with any more of her sister's probing, no matter how well intentioned. She'd long ago come to terms with the fact that she was different, but the painful learning process was vividly etched in her mind, leaving her gun-shy.

Who would believe that having an IQ in the genius range could be such a headache—or cause so much misery? Stephanie had learned early in life to withstand the cruel taunts of her young classmates who hadn't known how to deal with someone so different from themselves. And later, from classmates much older than she, had come the subtle whispers of "nerd," "freak"—or worse.

She'd learned to endure the rejection, or at least she'd tried. In the end she'd simply closed herself off from everyone save a select few, at times secretly wondering if allowing those childish jeers to hurt somehow made her weak. She was wise enough to realize that perhaps there were others with her peculiarity who handled it with more aplomb.

What stood out most in her memory was the loneliness—the isolation—as if she had nothing in common with another human being.

There had always been someone around who wanted to make use of her talent, emphasizing her difference, isolating her from her peers, separating her from the rest of the world.

She'd always wanted a large family—people she could love and who would love her, accept her for herself. Like Alex always had. Jason had been a start. But it didn't look like she was doing such a good job for him.

Had she made a mistake having Jason the way she had? Should she have waited, hoping that the "right man" might come along? But she hadn't had that option. If she had waited, she never would have had Jason or any child.

Climbing the stairs, Stephanie concentrated on the numerous paintings, from oil to watercolor, that ascended the wall beside her. They seemed to echo the loneliness. The pictures were all beautiful, but impersonal. And the way they were hung—grouped here and throughout the house—was more in keeping with a public gallery than a private residence.

After years of agonizing, she'd finally come to realize that, without meaning to, she made others feel inferior, highlighting their own insecurities or spawning their envy. She understood—but understanding didn't lessen the hurt.

As far back as she could remember, she'd done what was expected of her. She still could hear her father's voice. *Stephanie, you've been given a special gift. It's your responsibility to use it to its fullest potential.*

And she'd complied, to please him and her mother, hoping against hope that they would notice the person beneath the brains. Notice that she wasn't a robot, a machine to simply do what was expected of her. But she'd finally learned that that had been all either of her parents wanted of her. Neither had seemed to care that there was a vulnerable girl inside who craved acceptance and love like everyone else.

Well, she'd had enough of doing what was expected of her. She was through allowing herself to be exploited to further someone else's dream, someone else's ambition. And as soon as she finished her current project, she intended to pursue her dream of writing full-time. No one else was going to manipulate her. Or use her.

And her first order of business, she decided, was to find a place that was more homey. Architecturally, this house was perfection; aesthetically, it was exquisite. But it had no soul. Her parents had built it when she was quite young, for the singular purpose of showcasing their extensive collection of artwork. They'd succeeded in creating a museum, but not much of a home.

Still, it had been the family residence before her parents' deaths, and until recently, Stephanie had wanted to hold onto it. Alex had lived here all her life, while she had lived here only between school sessions. But it had represented the one constant in her otherwise vagabond childhood.

Her bare feet padded silently along the gleaming, pickled-hardwood floor, past the door to Alex's rooms on the left. As she passed Jason's rooms, she heard faint sounds that indicated he'd given up his book in favor of his computer. She shook her head. She almost wished he wasn't quite so fascinated by it. She wanted him to do what other seven-year-old boys did, whatever that was.

Reaching the last door on the corridor, she opened it and entered a large room that served as her office. She continued through to the bedroom and into the bath, shedding clothing as she went.

This was her sanctuary, her refuge from the outside world. Carefully chosen oriental rugs added warmth as well as beauty. She'd selected furniture that invited a person to relax and linger awhile. With vibrant shades of turquoise and muted hues of gray, she'd created an inviting oasis not reflected elsewhere in the house. But the usual tranquillity eluded her today.

Images of Nick Saxon and the effect he'd had on her kept playing through her mind. Her reaction to him had been immediate, electric—and overwhelming. It had caught her off guard. The last thing she needed, she reminded herself firmly, was to be harboring romantic ideas about this man. She knew that would only lead to heartache.

Yet she recognized, on some basic feminine level, that in this case the attraction was mutual.

The unbidden thought brought her to a stop. Nick was the kind of man who allowed none of his emotions to show. So where had that idea come from? Shaking her head, she decided her usually overactive imagination must be working overtime.

Stepping into the shower, she ignored the hot water in favor of head-clearing cold. It helped only marginally. Several minutes later she returned to the bedroom and slipped into a loose-fitting, seafoam green jumpsuit. Toweling her hair, she wandered over to the wall of windows opposite her English canopy bed, scarcely noticing the serene view of the secluded grounds and the shimmering reflecting pool.

Jason's eagerness to strike up a friendship with Nick had caught her off guard as well. It was the most enthusiasm her son had shown in some time for anything outside his usual routine. On one hand, that pleased her. Being around a male role model who appeared to share some of her opinions might be good for Jason.

And Nick certainly seemed more than willing. The two of them had hit it off right from the beginning.

But on the other hand, she wasn't certain she wanted Nick as Jason's role model. At times he seemed so intense. And there were still too many unanswered questions about him. There were depths to him that she was certain no one was allowed to plumb.

Sliding open the massive glass door, Stephanie stepped out onto the private balcony. How vulnerable would she be, she couldn't help wondering, when Nick got to know her? How vulnerable would that make Jason?

There was little she wouldn't do for her son. Jason had always been an undemanding child. Perhaps too much so. In fact, this was the first time he had demanded anything.

She'd known when she'd decided to have a child that being a single parent wouldn't be easy, that there would be problems, obvious and unforeseen. And she'd been right. Raising a son alone was far from easy. She realized she needed a man's input.

But could she trust Nick? What would be the repercussions if he discovered the circumstances of her son's birth? But then again, she questioned silently, how would he find out? It wasn't something that generally came up in conversation. *And how did you get pregnant? Oh, I went to the local fertility clinic and purchased a specimen from an anonymous donor.*

Stephanie sighed philosophically. She was being ridiculous. At this stage she really didn't have a choice. Jason had extracted a promise from her to let Nick coach him.

The next time she saw Nick, she'd make an appointment for a swim lesson.

Having come to terms with her decision, she allowed the soft strains of music drifting through the open doorway to wash over her. A few minutes later she headed back inside to her office. On the walls, intermingled with vivid tapestries and knotted hangings, were dozens of photographs of Jason and Alex taken on family outings. Scattered among them were sketches of what other worlds might look like—sketches that lent a whimsical touch to the very personal room.

In one corner, next to a window smaller than those in her bedroom, sat her computer. Dropping into the comfortable desk chair, Stephanie turned the machine on. When it beeped, she called up a locked, coded file, accessible only to herself. As the words appeared on the screen in front of her, she felt the familiar excitement.

This was the other joy of her life. One she didn't share with anyone.

The insistent ring of the telephone finally forced Nick from the soothing comfort of a warm shower. Three times in a row the caller had hung up before the answering machine could click in. Evidently, whoever was on the other end wasn't going to give up. Nick grabbed a towel and headed for his bedside phone, snatching up the receiver on the fourth ring.

"Saxon."

"Sorry to bother you, Nick."

The voice of his superior was not a welcome sound. "I don't want to talk to you, Matt. I'm on leave."

"No, you're not," Matt reminded him gently, amusement lacing his words. "We're just allowing you to play charades for a while."

"I didn't realize I'd have you breathing down my neck." Though Nick's words were wryly humorous, his tone had a slight edge. Any other time he would have welcomed the interruption from his old friend and colleague. But right now he had far more important things on his mind.

"The guys on the next rung up expect periodic updates."

"Hell, Matt, this is a cover. What's to report?"

"True. But there *is* an ongoing investigation underway at that lab, even if you're not officially part of it. I went out on a limb for you," his friend reminded him. "My butt's on the line. So's yours."

"Yeah, I know." Nick released a breath. "Thanks."

There was a pause. "Just wanted to remind you that you're treading on dangerous ground."

"I've been doing that for a long time."

"Be careful."

"Yeah, right." Funny, Nick suddenly realized, how he no longer wanted to take the risks he'd taken routinely for so many years.

"I wouldn't bother you if it wasn't important."

"Like hell you wouldn't," he said succinctly, a smile shadowing his mouth.

"How long before you think you'll be ready to come back to the real world?"

This meant trouble, Nick knew. "What's up?"

"We've got a problem."

He muttered an oath under his breath and rubbed the back of his neck in frustration. "Okay, give it to me."

All traces of humor left Matt's voice. "Our contact informs me that the buyer will be coming in earlier than we expected."

"How much earlier?"

"I'm not sure yet. Just wanted to alert you."

"What the hell happened? Last I heard, these guys would take weeks to scare up enough money for a buy this big." And he desperately needed those weeks to get to know his son.

"That's what our best intelligence sources indicated. Apparently our 'friends' have found a sponsor."

"You'd better find more reliable sources. This little slip up could be critical." To the organization. To his partner. To him.

"I agree. And we're working on it. As soon as I know anything concrete, I'll get back to you."

"I don't need this right now, Matt," Nick told him flatly.

"You're our best man, Nick. You're key to the operation. We don't have another alternative."

"Damn it, the agency is not the most important thing in my life," he shot back. A few weeks ago, he realized, they would have laughed at the irony of that assertion.

"I know, Nick, and I'm sorry."

"How soon?" The words held resignation. Nick knew he couldn't back out at this critical point.

"Don't know yet. But it's going down a lot quicker than any of us anticipated." The sympathetic quality had left Matt's voice. What remained was unyielding command. "Be ready."

Before Nick could tell his friend—and boss—where he could stick it, Matt severed the connection.

Damn, but the timing was lousy. Nick couldn't afford to be pulled away from his son before he'd had a chance to get acquainted with him, to establish himself in Jason's life. He absently walked over to the bedroom window and stared out into the darkening night.

He was under the gun now. Time was critical. He'd have to charm his way past Stephanie's defenses. Frankly, he wasn't used to a woman unattached and over twenty-one being this standoffish around him. It wasn't that he expected all females to fall at his feet. Ordinarily he wouldn't have given Stephanie's coolness a second thought. The number of women who'd regularly thrown themselves at him over the years since Sally's death had caused him to develop a certain cynicism toward the opposite sex. If a woman wasn't interested in him romantically, his ego could handle it. In fact, it was often a relief. But this time the stakes were higher than a casual date or sexual liaison.

His stock-in-trade was putting people at ease, getting them to open up. Few even realized that he was ferreting out tidbits of information, deliberately gaining their trust. That was necessary in undercover work. And he'd become very proficient at it.

He hoped to hell he hadn't overestimated his ability when it came to Dr. Stephanie Harcourt.

Nick carried a steaming, homemade pizza from the kitchen out to the flagstone patio. A gleaming swimming pool dominated the enclosed yard in back of his Tudor-style farmhouse. The latest swimming lesson had ended when he'd suggested lunch to Stephanie and a ravenous Jason. It seemed his son was always hungry, Nick thought, smiling inwardly.

Placing the food on the opaque glass table, he glanced over at Stephanie. She was standing a few feet away, intently watching Jason, who was still frolicking in the water. Nick had noted during three separate visits that Stephanie spent more time out of the water than in it. Just why, he couldn't say.

Try as he might, he couldn't deny the fact that Stephanie genuinely loved her son. And she was concerned for his happiness. He'd witnessed both on more than one occasion over the last several days. It would be a hell of a lot easier to dislike her if she weren't such a dedicated parent.

While she was preoccupied, Nick allowed his gaze to skim down the length of her. He wondered if she was aware that the almost indecently skimpy bathing suits so many women favored these days couldn't begin to compete with the conservative, strapless one-piece that hugged every line and curve of her own sleek figure. That was probably because her suit tantalized and teased at what was hidden beneath the shiny, turquoise fabric. It was just the thing to stimulate his naturally inquisitive mind.

Not to mention another far more primitive part of his anatomy. And he was certain beyond doubt that this was not the reaction the good doctor was striving for. He swore silently.

He allowed his gaze to drift down Stephanie's body again. Her lithe form showed no signs that she'd once carried a baby. *His* baby. The unbidden image triggered a visceral possessiveness that disturbed him.

Damn! Grabbing her beach jacket from a chair, he walked up behind her and draped it over her back. She jerked slightly in surprise, and he settled his hands on her shoulders, absorbing the fine tension in her. Knowing that he had that effect on her didn't help him rein in his own rioting senses. He took a half step closer, his body almost touching hers. "You're going to burn."

His gruff words, whispered a hairbreadth from her ear, seemed to hold an erotic promise. It aroused a delicious melting sensation in Stephanie. Instinctively she leaned against him. "B-burn?"

"You've been in the sun all morning—" he stroked his palms down her now-covered arms "—without using much sunscreen." He eased her around to face him, capturing and holding her gaze.

Stephanie's entire body responded to his touch, his tone. A seductive weakness seeped into her limbs. Her lips parted involuntarily.

There was the faintest hint of moisture on them, left by the nervous foray of her tongue. Nick silently groaned. He wondered if she had any idea just how badly he wanted to taste her. Would she be coolly remote or warmly receptive? To find out, all he had to do was lower his head just a few inches....

Jason's loud squeals from the pool shattered the spell. Nick muttered an oath under his breath and stepped back from Stephanie, feeling a momentary stab of conscience. She looked as rattled as he felt. Damn. It wasn't his style to stampede a woman. Particularly this woman. Behind her unsophisticated directness he sensed vulnerability and deep distrust.

He experienced a rare moment of confusion. He was always in control—of himself, of his emotions. Or had been until recently.

Stephanie allowed him to guide her over to a table shaded by a large umbrella. He seated her in one of the thickly padded chairs. Taking the chair next to her, he poured them each a glass of iced tea.

She declined his offer of pizza. Food was the last thing she wanted at the moment. Nick had pulled on a shirt earlier, without bothering to button it. His efficient movements kept revealing glimpses of bare chest, textured with a smattering of dark hair. Though he'd been bare-chested all morning as he coached Jason, she found herself experiencing a burning curiosity to run her hands inside the thin barrier of cloth. She picked up her glass, deliberately squashing the impulse.

"So, tell me about your Ph.D." Nick picked up a slice of pizza and took a bite.

"What do you want to know?" she asked, disconcerted by his abrupt change in mood and topic. At the moment she felt ill-equipped to handle any conversation, much less this one.

He shrugged. "What's your degree in?" He took a bite of pizza.

"Mathematics," she said, then deliberately added, "for one."

"And?" he prompted around another mouthful.

She toyed with her glass of tea, wondering where this was going. "Physics." For someone without an ounce of fat on his body, he certainly had a healthy appetite. Reminded her a little of Jason, when he sat down long enough to eat.

Nick nodded, polishing off the last of his pizza with consummate ease, then pushed his plate aside. "And?"

He was concentrating solely on her now. "Several foreign languages." She wished she could tell what he was thinking, but his expression remained unreadable. Across the expanse of flagstone, her gaze sought out Jason, still chasing through the water. Best to lay all her cards on the table, she told herself, and see just how far and how fast this man would run.

"Let's see if I can make this clear. To put it as delicately as I can, I'm probably smarter than you. My IQ is off the scales. I'm going to understand things quicker than you, concepts that most people have a hard time grasping. That's the way it is." She raised her chin a notch. "And I can't pretend otherwise."

Instead of looking shocked by her outburst, Nick continued to watch her steadily. "What makes you think," he asked evenly, "that I'd be put off by an intelligent woman?"

Feeling slightly chagrined, she smiled wryly. "Because, in my experience, most men are." It had taken her many years to finally accept who and what she was. She wasn't bitter, but she prided herself on being a realist.

"Tell me something." He propped his elbows on the table, then waited until her eyes met his. "Are you a snob?"

Her chin came up another notch. "Of course not." She hadn't meant to sound condescending.

He lifted an eyebrow. "Do you have trouble talking with someone who's not as smart as you?"

Defensive anger came to her rescue. "Are you saying that you're not as smart as I am?"

Nick grinned, letting her sarcasm roll off him. "Then why bring up the subject of IQs?"

The question was logical—and took the wind out of her sails. Well, she thought ironically, this is the second time he's put me in my place. But she'd been down this road too many times to accept his evasion. "Simply trying to be honest." She picked up the paper napkin next to her untouched plate and began to pleat it into tiny rows.

"Are you?"

She eyed him carefully, trying to read what was behind his dark gaze. "Generally speaking, most men are gone quicker than lightning when confronted by an overly intelligent female." Unless, of course, they had a *use* for her.

"Are you suggesting I can't handle dealing with you?" he countered, amusement in his expression.

She was out of her depth. Clever give-and-take with a man as arrogant as Nick Saxon was not her forte. She took a deep breath and decided a strategic retreat was in order. "Please don't misunderstand. I just don't want Jason to get his hopes up, only to be disappointed."

Or herself, Nick silently added. He sensed that she'd been hurt. And the sense of outrage he experienced on her behalf caught him by surprise. Hell. This was going to be trickier than he'd imagined.

"I don't think I'm that shallow, Stephanie. Why don't you let me decide what turns me off—or on?" he said softly. "I may not have your IQ, but I do have a good mind and I'm content with it."

He didn't seem angry, which Stephanie found little short of astonishing, considering that she'd just finished insulting the man.

"Look, I'd like to be Jason's friend." He studied her with cool eyes. "Yours, too, if you'll let me." And he found he really meant it.

That would be a novel experience, Stephanie thought, and a suspicious corner of her mind wanted to ask him why. But she didn't. Instead she simply nodded, refusing to look away from his dark, assessing eyes. If she wasn't careful, Nick Saxon was going to slip right past all her carefully constructed barriers. And that would leave her exposed to the old, familiar pain.

"Hey, Nick!" Jason shouted from the pool, breaking the tension between the two adults. "Is lunch ready yet?"

"Yeah," he called back, without taking his eyes from Stephanie's. "Come and get it."

"Great!" Jason swam for the side of the pool.

Stephanie pressed a hand over the disturbing flutter in her stomach, but she could think of nothing further to say in explanation or defense.

"Tell you what," Nick said. "I've always favored the direct approach. I like Jason and he seems to like me. I think I might be able to help him. Why don't we relax and see where this goes?"

Stephanie searched his harsh features, gauging his sincerity. Was she foolish to trust him? "All right." She needed a moment to regroup. She stood to go inside, but he snagged her wrist with one strong hand.

His voice took on a smooth edge. "Shocking as this may seem to you, I find being around you very... stimulating." She tried to free her arm, but his fingers tightened. "You have my word," he said quietly. "I won't hurt Jason."

"Thank you."

Still he didn't release her. "Something else you should remember." Once again he waited for her to look at him. "I'm not most men. Don't pretend with me," he added, referring to her earlier statement about being unable to pretend she wasn't a genius. "Ever."

He shrugged off the momentary jab of conscience that struck him. It was good advice and he meant it. But considering the deception he was practicing with her, what did that make him?

Surprised, Stephanie nodded once, and his hand dropped away from her arm. She'd detected unshakable determination in his grip. It convinced her, however foolishly, that this was a man who would do nothing he didn't *choose* to do.

Nick's gaze followed her as she hurried through the French doors into the house. He hoped to hell he'd be able to keep his word. One thing was certain. Stephanie didn't have a prayer in hell of scaring him off. And not simply because of Jason.

Far from being put off by her mind, Nick found himself fascinated by it. As much as he'd cared for Sally, she hadn't been intellectually stimulating. She'd been content with the traditional roles of wife and mother, though, through no fault of her own, she'd never had an opportunity to try the latter.

Stephanie challenged him on several levels, no question about that. But not in a negative sense, as she apparently assumed. She was the first woman who'd piqued his interest since his wife's death. Or maybe ever. He felt a prickle of disloyalty that Stephanie was the first woman to overshadow Sally.

Jason bounded up the wide brick steps leading from the pool apron to the flagstone patio, raining droplets of chlorinated water as he came. Nick threw him a towel, hungrily studying his son.

When had he come to love Jason beyond measure?

When had he decided that he would be a part of Jason's life, no matter what the cost?

Chapter Four

Stephanie opened the lab door and stepped inside. Nick was already at his desk—no, *her* desk, she amended silently, the one he'd commandeered his first day in *her* lab. She sighed. After yesterday, she knew she was treading on dangerous ground around this man.

"Good morning," he said, not looking away from his computer monitor.

"Morning." She reached for her lab coat and slipped it on over her mauve linen slacks and matching silk blouse. "How's the investigation coming?"

"Slowly."

"Uncovered anything of interest?"

Nick glanced over his shoulder at her, trying to gauge the odd note in her voice. "Not much." He leaned back in the chair and swiveled to face her. "The unauthorized accesses are random. I don't find a discernible pattern to them. No sabotage. Overall, the whole thing doesn't make sense." Overall, the whole thing seemed almost amateurish, he thought. But he didn't say it aloud.

Well, that was short and sweet. She picked up a stack of computer printouts and sifted through them. "Any new incidents?"

He propped his elbows on the arms of the chair, studying her over the steeple of his fingers. "No. But I think whoever's doing the hacking is on the inside."

She glanced up sharply from the papers in her hand. "Inside? Any idea who?"

"Not yet, but I'm working on it."

Clamping down on her agitation, Stephanie walked over to her own desk. She wanted this man out of her life. Fast. "Do you think you'll have something soon?"

He shrugged, still watching her much as a scientist would study a laboratory specimen. "I have no idea."

She tossed the papers aside. "I thought you were the best."

Nick smiled crookedly. "Is that a compliment?"

"I'm just wondering when I can get my lab back," she said, rearranging another stack of computer printouts.

"What's bothering you this morning?" he asked quietly.

She couldn't very well tell him that he was systematically dismantling each of her defenses, that she had the urgent feeling she needed to get him out of her life at the earliest possible moment. "Isn't there some way to speed this up?"

"These things take time. Honey, you need to get out of this lab and into the real world."

His words pushed her mood from beyond just frayed nerves into real irritation. "Thank you so much for your suggestion, Mr. Saxon. I'll keep it in mind." She reshuffled the stack of papers. "Of course, that's what I'm trying to do. But having you underfoot serves to slow down the process!"

Nick laughed outright. "So you're saying I'm a distraction?"

It was the first time she'd seen him laugh, and the sight of his face softened in genuine amusement made her heart somersault. Her reaction angered her, but not for the world would she let him know. She schooled her features into the prim mask she'd used so effectively over the years. "There's no doubt you're a distraction, but not the kind you seem to have in mind."

"This sounds interesting. What do I have in mind?"

She'd done it again—walked right into his trap. "How long am I going to have to put up with you?" she persisted.

He sobered then, turning back to the computer and shutting it down. "As long as it takes." He stood and began collecting his things. "Don't forget we have a date Wednesday."

"It's not a date," she stated firmly, feeling like a teenager. "Just a swimming lesson for Jason."

"Is it?" Again he grinned, moving toward the door. "We'll see." He waved and walked out.

Stephanie stared out one of the tall windows that framed the massive stone fireplace in Nick's chestnut-paneled family room. The wash of plump raindrops over the diamond-shaped, leaded-glass panes distorted her view. The storm, which had interrupted Nick and Jason's morning swim, was one of those sudden summer showers that cleansed the air of pollutants, making everything fresh and new again—until the infamous D.C. mugginess returned with a vengeance.

The hum of a computer and the *beeps, glucks* and *dings* of a fast-paced game in progress, mixed with frequent masculine yelps of triumph or dismay, told Stephanie that Jason was giving Nick a run for his money while they waited out the downpour. She found it a pleasant mixture of sounds. Smiling to herself, she wondered if her devious son had mentioned to Nick that he was considered a master at this particular game. Not that Nick seemed to mind. He hadn't once lost his good-natured acceptance of being routinely bested by a seven-year-old.

She turned to watch them. They were sitting in front of the computer monitor, heads almost touching. Jason's hair was several shades lighter than Nick's, but every bit as thick and unruly. Maybe it had something to do with male hair in general. Of course, never having been in a position to closely study a man's hair before, she couldn't say for certain. They looked so natural together, Stephanie reflected—almost like a family. The thought stirred a poignant longing in her.

Watching the two of them together reminded Stephanie how much she owed Nick. He seemed genuinely to enjoy having Jason around. They'd formed a close friendship in only a matter of days. And her son was thriving under Nick's easygoing companionship. Jason had begun to ease up on himself. For that alone she was enormously relieved and grateful.

Analyzing her own relationship with Nick wasn't so easy. He had a way of drawing her out. And she had a habit of blurting out things to him that she didn't reveal to another soul. But nothing she said or did seemed to shock him or throw him off balance. If she'd thought she could discourage the man, she'd been sadly disillusioned. Nothing seemed to faze him.

Or had it? Over the last several days, though he'd made her feel welcome, she'd detected a certain reserve in him. There'd been no clever innuendos or teasing remarks. She frowned slightly as a new thought struck her. Because of her own insecurities, had she learned to reject others before they could reject her? Was she at least partly to blame for her own loneliness?

Was it possible that this man was different?

She shied away from the idea. Experience had taught her that men always wanted something from her. And it usually had something to do with the use of her intellectual abilities. One time years ago she'd allowed herself to believe otherwise, and she'd opened her heart to a fellow classmate whom she thought cared for her. She'd given him her body only to discover that it was her mind he was really interested in. The irony of that painful episode hadn't left her.

So what did Nick Saxon want? She rubbed her arms to ward off the sudden chill that scurried through her. Maybe she was becoming paranoid.

Her life had always been so predictable—placid and regimented—until Nick Saxon had entered it. What shook her most, she acknowledged, was the sensual awareness that overpowered her common sense whenever he came within arm's reach. From their first meeting she'd felt an inexplicable connection with him—something she'd never experienced before.

Which perhaps explained the erotic, somewhat frightening fantasies Nick roused in her. More than one night they'd caused her to toss and turn for hours in a bed that was becoming a sensual prison. She felt the warm pooling of tension deep inside and wrapped her arms tighter across her midriff.

Nick Saxon, a tiny voice warned, threatened her safe, albeit dull, world on some fundamental level.

Through the large kitchen windows Nick watched the dispersing dark clouds play tag with a watery sun. His gaze returned to Stephanie. With Jason's help, she was making sandwiches.

Each time she moved, the loose cover-up she'd pulled on displayed enticing glimpses of the sleek, figure-hugging bathing suit beneath. As with all her others, the suit covered far more than it revealed. And, as usual, it made keeping his thoughts from wandering into forbidden territory damned difficult. He ordered himself to concentrate on setting out the few utensils needed for the light lunch. He had an idea that she'd lose her newly acquired relaxed manner if she became aware of his frank, masculine appraisal. The last thing he needed was to trigger her wariness again.

He'd never imagined Stephanie at work in his kitchen—or any kitchen, for that matter. Even in a bathing suit, she always looked so elegant, so prim and proper, as if someone should be waiting on her. After all, someone as busy as she, with live-in help available round the clock, wouldn't be expected to know the difference between a microwave oven and a food processor. But she knew her way around. And she'd obviously taught Jason the rudimentary functions of a kitchen. They both fit naturally into the cozy, domestic scene. Nick felt a sharp ache.

"Here you go, Jason," Stephanie said, handing him a plate of sandwiches. "Put these on the table."

Jason carefully carried the plate over to the solid cherry table that dominated the kitchen eating area.

"Nick," he asked, setting down his burden and climbing onto a chair, "do you think I can swim faster yet?"

"Let's not jump the gun here, champ," Nick cautioned, pulling up the chair beside his son. "We've only been at it a couple of weeks." As part of their original deal, he'd purposely banned the use of a stopwatch. He'd wanted the boy to ease up and simply learn to enjoy himself.

"But how will I know if I'm getting any better? I've been practicing forever," he grumbled.

"First we concentrate on getting the strokes right, then we worry about times. Isn't that what we agreed?"

"I guess so." The words were offered grudgingly, but the look on Jason's face said eloquently he wasn't sure that had been wise.

"There are a couple of other things I want to try before we start competing against the clock."

"Like what?" Renewed eagerness entered Jason's voice.

"Well, a swimmer's greatest strength comes from his shoulder muscles."

"Yeah?"

"So I suggest we work on those next."

"How do we do that?" Jason asked.

We. Nick's heart seemed to swell inside his chest, causing a bittersweet ache. He and his son had formed a strong bond in the short time they'd been working together. But Nick wanted more. So much more. He wanted to be able to talk to his son about things other than swimming—like what he'd been told about his father. And if he ever wondered about his dad.

"Best way I know to build up shoulder muscles is on a sailboat."

"Have you got a sailboat?" Eagerness bloomed into genuine excitement.

Nick chuckled. "Sure do. Are you interested?"

"Yeah! When can we go?"

"Go where?" Stephanie asked. She'd gone to the pantry for a pitcher and had missed part of the discussion. Placing lemonade on the table, she seated herself as far from Nick as possible. Being too close to him, she'd learned, had a way of interfering with her rational thinking.

"Can we go out on Nick's boat?"

"Boat?"

A flicker of some emotion that Nick couldn't quite catch clouded Stephanie's golden green eyes. "You don't like boats?" he asked.

"Well—" she frowned slightly "—not exactly."

"Then what, exactly?" Nick probed.

"You see, I . . ." Stephanie hesitated.

"Mom can't swim," Jason said around a bite of sandwich.

Of all the possible reservations Stephanie might have had, this one would never have occurred to Nick. His first impulse was to laugh at the joke. Everybody knew how to swim, right? Certainly someone with her background would have learned. But one look at Stephanie's shuttered features told him that wasn't the case. Well, hell, he thought. That would explain the frustration he'd sensed in her that first day at the swim meet. If she didn't know how to swim, she'd have difficulty identifying with Jason's problems. It also explained why she rarely went near the water. "You really can't swim?"

"'Fraid not." Stephanie found confirming the answer embarrassing. It was another personal detail she'd rather didn't become public knowledge. In fact, she hadn't realized Jason knew; but then her son was nothing if not perceptive.

Nick gave Stephanie a lopsided smile. "Wonder what other secrets I could learn about you from Jason?"

"I sincerely hope that's the first and the last," Stephanie said dryly. She shot Jason a playful glare and reached over to nudge him in the ribs. "Traitor. Don't think I won't remember this." Her son had a wonderfully sly sense of humor that sneaked out from time to time when least expected. It was an endearing quality, usually. Today, however, Stephanie could cheerfully strangle him because of it.

"Aw, Mom." Jason tried to look sheepish but instead burst into giggles. "It's only the truth."

Stephanie handled the boy well, Nick again acknowledged—with just the right amount of concern tempered with tolerance, encouragement without pressure. The gentle teasing between mother and son struck a tender cord in him. Even though it was something he, too, shared with Jason, seeing Stephanie and his son together somehow made Nick feel excluded.

Watching them reminded him just how empty his life had been for so many years. He'd always been a loner, even in his large family. Sally had been able to fill some of the gaps, but never the deepest parts of him. He'd never minded before. Why did it bother him now?

He scanned Stephanie's flushed features. "There's nothing to worry about. I make sure all my passengers wear life jackets."

"Well, you see, Mom doesn't like—" Jason began.

Stephanie held up her hand for silence. "Thanks, but I can fight my own battles."

"Jason, why don't you go practice one of those computer games?" Nick suggested, sensing Stephanie's chagrin. "I think I'm about to catch up with you."

"I know. You two want to talk." Jason heaved a long-suffering sigh and looked from his mother to Nick. "Grown-ups!" he grumbled as he trudged from the kitchen.

Stephanie's sensation of abandonment was strong. She was acutely conscious of Nick's probing watchfulness, like a big jungle cat who'd cornered his prey.

"Boats make me...uneasy," she offered as soon as Jason had left the room.

"Uh-huh." Scared silly was more like it. Nick studied her for several heartbeats, a smile softening one corner of his mouth. "That can be remedied."

"Oh, no," she stated categorically, immediately catching on to what his "remedy" would be. "I don't want to learn to swim."

"Sure you do."

"I do?"

Nick nodded. "You'd feel a hell of a lot less apprehensive when Jason's swimming."

A shadow flickered in her eyes. "I can't argue with that."

He leaned forward, resting his forearms on the edge of the table. "There's another reason."

Below his rolled-up sleeves his arms were lean and sinewy and deeply tanned. And strong. If they held her, Stephanie was certain there was little she would fear. The fleeting thought stunned her. She cleared her throat. "Yes?"

"I want you," he said, a teasing light entering his dark eyes, "to look forward to our outings."

His close proximity was making Stephanie feel ridiculously breathless. "Don't you think it's rather late for me to learn to swim?"

"The way I look at it," he said, some of the teasing leaving his voice, "it's never too late to go after what you want."

Stephanie felt the vibrations roll through her, stirring sensations she still wondered if it was safe for her to feel. He continued to hold her gaze, and she refused to look away. She was certain he would take that as an indication of weakness. It seemed very important at this moment that he not discover her weakness.

"I'll teach you. All you need," Nick said softly, "is the courage to go for it."

Though he hadn't moved, she couldn't shake the feeling that he was closing in on her. A little desperately, she tried a different tact. "I wouldn't want to take up any more of your time."

His gaze strayed down her body, taking in the white swimsuit showing beneath her coverup. While the suit wasn't overly snug, it didn't conceal the outline of her erect nipples. It took all his willpower to lift his gaze back to her face. "Someone with your obvious... talents shouldn't take all that much."

At first she thought he was mocking her, but nothing in his demeanor confirmed that. She picked up a napkin and restlessly folded it into a geometric design. Whether wise or not, it seemed she was going to have to tell him the truth. "It's a little more complicated than that."

"Oh?" he said encouragingly.

"I'm scared to death of deep water."

He hadn't anticipated her candor. It touched something inside him, and he ground his teeth. He didn't want to admire her. He didn't want to care about her fears or her hopes or her dreams. God, this situation was crazy. Initially all he'd wanted was to get to his son. He hadn't gotten around to deciding what came next.

And he knew, he *knew*, that he had to remain objective. But he needed to gain her trust. And he needed an excuse, any excuse, to keep coming around. Teaching Stephanie to swim was as good as any. He'd be a fool not to use it, he told himself, even as his conscience kicked in.

Why couldn't she have been an unfit mother or a workaholic or someone who acted as if her child was a possession? It would have made things a hell of a lot easier for him to treat her like any other obstacle in his way. But she was none of those. She was dedicated and caring and wanted what was best for Jason.

And he was beginning to feel an aching empathy with her. What few glimpses she'd allowed into her life revealed a lonely existence. And that he understood. He'd been there. Hell, he *was* there.

His guilt was slowly being overshadowed by a new concern. If Stephanie discovered his hidden agenda, how would it affect her?

Damn it, he couldn't afford to allow his unexpected concern for her to interfere with his ultimate goal. "You've trusted me to work with Jason."

It was this second challenge that did it. Despite her fear of water, Stephanie experienced an exhilarating rush of excitement—something she seldom allowed herself. For the first time in she couldn't remember when, she felt daring. She deliberately disregarded the tiny voice in her head whispering that entrusting her son to this man wasn't remotely similar to entrusting herself.

"All right," she said with a quiet dignity that spoke of breeding and years of self-discipline, "you have yourself a pupil."

"Good. We'll start Sunday morning."

She looked out at the sunlight glinting off the crystalline blue water of the pool several yards beyond the patio. "Why not right now?" she asked, afraid she might lose her nerve.

He shook his head slowly from side to side. "Today we have an audience. Sunday it will be just you and me...no other distractions." That he'd like nothing better than to be alone with her, he assured himself, had nothing to do with it. While a rational part of his mind tried to convince him that was true, a much more spontaneous part of his body forced him to acknowledge the lie that it was.

"Oh. Well." She laid a hand over her stomach to suppress the sensual flutter before she made a fool of herself. She was being ridiculous. The man was going to teach her to swim—not seduce her. "You're the teacher."

He felt a rush of triumph at the same moment he realized he was entering delicate territory. This woman had private hurts that she hid carefully and didn't talk about easily. But he was finding that he wanted to know more—to uncover all the secrets of Stephanie Harcourt. She may have agreed to let him teach her to swim, but he knew her trust was tentative at best.

If she were to suddenly suspect that he wasn't being completely honest with her, he didn't doubt for a minute that her trust would be nonexistent.

Chapter Five

Stephanie fingered the leather-clad passenger door of Alex's black Mercedes, barely registering the bright, hazy morning. "You'll pick me up at two o'clock?" she asked again.

"Right on the button." Alex glanced with raised brows at her older sister as the car idled in front of Nick's house. "Are you having second thoughts?"

She hesitated a fraction of a second, then squared her shoulders. "Of course not. I just don't want to impose on Nick's generosity."

Alex gave a very unladylike snort. "Right, Sis." Her expression became sympathetic. "I'll be happy to leave the car here for you. One of the guys from the precinct can pick me up."

"No. No." Stephanie had asked Alex to drop her off because she was afraid she'd never have made it this far on her own. Having a car available would provide too easy an avenue of escape. She was certainly fortunate, Stephanie inwardly mocked, to have a sister with a work schedule so flexible that she could serve as a private chauffeur.

Alex gave Stephanie's arm a reassuring squeeze. "If you decide you want to leave earlier, give me a call."

"Thanks." Stephanie opened the car door and stepped out onto the concrete pavement.

As if on cue, the walnut-stained front door of the Tudor house opened and Nick appeared. He folded his arms across his chest and leaned against the frame, his dark gaze tracking her, as if he could read her mind and knew she wanted nothing better than to turn tail and run.

She was mildly irritated with herself for noticing the way his casual stance pulled the knit shirt taut against his powerful shoulders. Its dark color served to underscore his imposing size—and the predatory aura about him. A pair of tight jeans hugged his hips lovingly and with obvious familiarity. She found keeping her gaze where polite society expected took a surprising amount of self-discipline.

Stephanie's slow ascent up the three flagstone steps onto the porch reminded Nick of someone on her way to an execution. "Right on time." He smiled crookedly. "Good, I like punctuality."

Lord, she thought, the man made the word sound downright erotic.

Pushing away from the doorjamb, he moved back to allow her to enter.

She stepped inside the cool hallway. This was the first time she'd been in Nick's home without Jason along. She found herself looking at it in an entirely new light.

"You have a very—" she groped for the right word "—pleasing home."

Amusement glinted in his dark eyes. "In other words, because I'm single, you expected a slob?"

"Oh, no." She seemed to have a problem lately with her wayward tongue; it kept engaging before her brain was in gear. "But now that you mention it, a big house doesn't seem to suit your life-style."

"No?" Nick raised a speculative brow. "What does?"

"I don't know. A high-rise condominium, maybe. Something chic and sophisticated." Something typical of a single male of the nineties, she added silently.

"I see. Bachelor digs."

"Maybe."

"Sometimes first impressions can be misleading," he said dryly. He'd bought the small farm just outside D.C. several years ago because it was located close enough to company headquarters so that he could easily drive in when needed, but far enough from the congestion of urban life to keep him from feeling closed in. He still had trouble handling anything that made him feel trapped. It was too vivid a reminder of the bamboo prison he'd had to survive during his last months in Nam.

It dawned on her that she was making unfair assumptions about him. She felt heat rise in her cheeks. "That was rude and I apologize." She cast an almost wistful glance around the shadowed hallway. Here there was a patina of warmth and caring—so different from her own home. "In fact, it's perfect—lots of character, warm, inviting."

"Thank you." His gaze searched her face for a moment. "You're right. A house this size should have a family." Something he'd figured he'd have long before he reached his forties. But fate had decreed otherwise. Or so he'd thought. "At times it can be a little lonely and a challenge for one person to keep up. But then," he added, "I've always liked challenges."

Nick cupped his hand under her elbow and ushered her farther inside. The door closed behind them.

"Would you like some breakfast before we get started?"

"No. Thank you."

"Coffee?"

"No. No." She was positive she'd embarrass them both if she tried to force anything past the knot in her stomach. "Let's just get it over with."

"You make it sound like you're on your way to an execution." She seemed so defenseless this morning, Nick thought, and just short of terrified. He'd never seen fear in her before. The immediate urge to pull her close and protect her from anything that might cause her distress caught him by surprise. He found his impulsive reaction disturbing.

She laughed nervously. "That about sums up my feelings right at the moment."

"I promise it'll be painless." He studied her a moment longer, deciding the best way to proceed. He'd pushed Stephanie into this as a means of coaxing her to loosen up some, maybe even gaining a small measure of her trust. Scaring her to death wasn't likely to accomplish either. "Let's go out by the pool and relax for a while."

Stephanie nodded and followed him, feeling immense relief, concentrating on the inviting, paneled rooms. They stepped out onto the flagstone patio and continued down the steps to the pool. It almost seemed out of place on the grounds of the seventy-odd-year-old structure.

"Would you like to use a guest room to change?"

She shook her head. "I have my suit on under my clothes."

At the innocent announcement, Nick felt the muscles in his stomach tighten. He tried not to envision what lay beneath her short jumpsuit.

Stephanie was grateful to have something to occupy her for a few minutes. And she was more than ready to shed the extra layer of material. The temperature was already creeping into the uncomfortable range, typical for August in Washington. She began shimmying out of the demure, Wedgwood blue jumpsuit, revealing a matching, figure-hugging swimsuit.

She felt slightly self-conscious. She'd chosen this particular suit because it was the only one she owned with straps. Since she didn't swim, they had never been a priority. But even with straps this suit afforded less coverage than any of her others. Alex had dared Stephanie to buy it. It had been another of her sister's attempts at changing Stephanie's rather prim image. Now, standing here in front of this man with nothing but the small amount of material covering her, she wondered if she'd chosen wisely. Get a grip, she lectured inwardly. The man was going to teach her to swim. He'd probably seen hundreds of women in bathing suits far more revealing than this.

To Nick the suit appeared the perfect choice for swimming—from the front. But the back was another story altogether. His breath caught somewhere between his lungs and his diaphragm. Crisscrossing delicate, gold straps held together almost nonexistent bits of fabric, exposing an indecent amount of bare skin.

The suit definitely wasn't one he'd have expected in this woman's wardrobe. It was at once demure and erotic and revealed another facet of Stephanie he hadn't anticipated.

He tamped down the fire that blazed to life low in his belly. She was here for a swimming lesson, he reminded himself. Period.

He watched her rummage through her carryall. After a few seconds she withdrew a bottle of sunscreen. "Could you help me with this, please?" She held out the container to him. "I hate to ask, but I can't reach my back. And if I don't use it, I'll resemble a lobster by noon."

Nick's gaze drifted slowly over the amount of creamy flesh vulnerable to the sun's rays and muttered an imprecation under his breath. She couldn't be that naive, he thought cynically. Or could she? Her expression held all the innocence of a fairy tale, and he realized with unexpected clarity that she hadn't a clue how she affected him.

He wasn't certain what annoyed him most—the fact that she turned him on to this degree or that she didn't notice. When was the last time he'd run into a woman who was unaware of being attractive as hell to the opposite sex?

He took the bottle from her outstretched hand. "Why not," he muttered, knowing he was making a mistake. But the invitation to touch her skin was far too tempting.

He gestured toward one of several brightly colored, padded lounge chairs. "Lie down."

The rusty sound of Nick's voice drew Stephanie's gaze to his face. His features were impassive save for the muscle that flexed in his hard jaw. An answering flutter tugged deep within her lower abdomen. *Don't let your imagination run away with you,* she warned herself. He was simply providing some friendly assistance. Depositing her jumpsuit on a small table, she walked over to the chair and carefully lay facedown on it.

He eased down beside her, feeling her thigh nestle intimately against his hip as his weight depressed the cushion. It sent another surge of heat straight to his groin.

Nick poured a good amount of the lotion into one palm and held it for several seconds, allowing the liquid to warm. Or was he putting off the inevitable? He knew what was going to happen to him as soon as he touched her.

He inhaled deeply and allowed the lotion to trickle onto her back before placing one hand on her sun-heated skin. With his other hand he slid aside the suit straps. Her back was beautiful, defined by delicately toned muscles. She shifted in a sinuous motion. And the tension in Nick's body increased another notch.

She was incredibly sexy in a subtle way—a way that lured a man closer while lulling him into a false sense of security. Dangerous. Very dangerous.

"Why don't you know how to swim?" Nick finally asked, redirecting his thoughts to something less volatile. "I'd expect the daughter of one of D.C.'s most prominent families to have every advantage."

"Oh, I guess because when most kids were old enough to learn, I was in one private school or another." Stephanie rested her chin on her folded arms, trying to block out the erotic designs Nick's warm hands were drawing on her skin. Though roughened by calluses, his palms were surprisingly gentle. And they were igniting an answering heat somewhere deep within her body.

"Don't they teach swimming in private school?"

She hesitated. "Of course. But I was... an unusual student."

Unusual. He didn't like the way she said the word. "How?"

"They—my parents—noticed that I was different when I was quite young. After it was established that my IQ was, shall we say, above average, they felt I should be given every opportunity to develop my potential. The schools they chose were instructed to explore that 'potential' to the fullest degree." She shifted again. "There was very little time for extracurricular activities."

"Such as swimming."

She nodded. Her teachers, mentors, even her parents had kept her wrapped in cotton, never allowing her to pursue anything that could conceivably injure her physically, until she'd felt stifled emotionally. She'd hated it, but there had been little she could do. Finally she'd stopped fighting and had yielded to the wishes of those in charge of her life.

"Why didn't you take lessons after you got out on your own?"

After a pause, she shrugged. "As I grew older I found it increasingly difficult to turn myself over to others to train, no matter what the discipline." It was one of the few ways she could protect what little independence she still possessed.

Nick sensed something else beneath the surface of what she was telling him. Something that a part of him, against his better judgment, wanted to explore. He switched directions. "What about friends?"

She shook her head. "No time. Every minute was filled with testing and experiments, learning and more learning."

There was no bitterness in her words. Only acceptance. She was an unusual woman. He wondered if under similar circumstances he would be quite so accommodating.

Since Sally's death he'd deliberately stayed away from women like Stephanie. Women who were honest and sincere—and had the right to demand much more from a man than straightforward, uncomplicated sex. He had nothing to offer a woman who would expect a commitment from a man. That had been taken from him eons ago in a jungle prison halfway around the world. Hadn't his sterility indirectly caused the death of his wife?

Trouble was, he'd decided he was bone tired of dealing with superficial women—the kind that seemed to dominate the Washington scene. And Stephanie Harcourt definitely wasn't in that category. Nor did she fit into the usual country-club set. There was no shallowness to her. No false pretenses. No exaggerated vanity.

"And your sister? When did she come along?" He sensed more than saw Stephanie smile.

"By the time she was born, I was away at a boarding school in upstate New York. I came home infrequently. In fact, I didn't even know Mother was expecting a baby until spring break. And there was Alex."

"You mean your parents didn't tell you? They just decided you didn't need to know such important family news?" he asked, feeling irritation on her behalf. Had they callously packed her away, excluding her from their lives? Like some poor relation, had she been tolerated when necessary and ignored the rest of the time?

She considered his question carefully before answering. "I suppose they felt it might interfere with my concentrating on my studies. At that time I was working on college-level courses."

Why in hell, he wondered, did he allow her poignant tale to bother him? His only interest here was his son. He was simply courting Stephanie as a means to that end. He had to remember that.

"Weren't there enough private schools around this area?"

"By then I'd outgrown what they could offer," she stated evenly. "Anyway, Alex was a wonderful surprise."

"You don't sound jealous of her."

"Of Alex? Heavens, no. I'd love to have had several siblings," she said wistfully. "I always wanted to be part of a large family."

"It has its advantages and disadvantages," Nick said mildly, thinking of his own family, which could be lovingly meddlesome on occasion, but boundlessly comforting in times of trouble.

"I was about ten when she was born and we hit it off right from the first." Stephanie sighed reminiscently and the small sound tugged at Nick. "I could get her to stop crying when Nanny and Mother were ready to throw their hands up in despair."

When she chuckled, Nick felt the vibrations run up his arms and threaten a spot inside him that had remained untouched for as long as he cared to remember. He removed his hands from her sleek, tantalizing back and grabbed the bottle of sunscreen. Time to work on her legs, he told himself firmly, gambling that they would be less arousing than her body.

Nick's hand on the back of her leg caused Stephanie to suck in a sharp breath.

"Sorry," he said huskily, realizing he'd gambled on the wrong odds. "I should've warmed the lotion first."

The intimate warmth of Nick's touch was causing the melting sensation inside Stephanie to expand in ever-widening circles. The long, lazy glide of his fingers up and down her thighs was making it hard for her to concentrate. His hands were pleasantly abrasive, setting off tiny explosions of erotic sensations.

"How often did you see her?"

See who? She was having difficulty recalling exactly what they'd been discussing. *Oh yes, Alex.* She swallowed, trying to relieve the sudden dryness in her throat. "I watched her grow up in blocks of time measured by school leaves and holidays. But that didn't keep us from becoming close."

Nick continued to stroke the smooth skin of Stephanie's long legs, not certain now whether to soothe or excite. Her sensuous movements beneath his hands stirred a very masculine satisfaction that he had the power to arouse her.

"Alex was so beautiful, with big green eyes and honey blond curls." Was that her voice? Stephanie wondered, amazed by the husky sound. She shifted, to get closer or farther away, she wasn't sure which. "And she always seemed to be glad to see me."

An image of a young girl with her nose pressed against the toy-store window formed in Nick's head. Irritation escalated into anger against her insensitive family. "I'm surprised she even knew who you were," Nick muttered under his breath.

Stephanie looked over her shoulder at Nick, puzzled at his grim expression. "What?"

"Nothing." He experienced a moment of guilt, wondering if the memories were painful to her. He didn't have a right to delve into Stephanie's personal life. He brushed the realization aside. "Go on."

"As she grew older, I started making up stories to tell her."

"Making them up? Why not just read to her?"

"That would have been too easy. I wanted to find a way to make her remember me while I was away. It had to be something no one else could do for her." Again Stephanie's chest rose as she chuckled. "And it worked. She was always excited to see me and couldn't wait to hear the latest fairy tale."

What Nick was discovering was a woman who'd learned to draw from inside herself to fill the emptiness in her life and in those around her. "Tell me about your stories."

He'd done it again, Stephanie thought in exasperation. Charmed her into telling him things she never discussed with anyone. She rolled away from him, pushing a silken fall of unruly bronze hair out of her eyes as she came to her feet and moved to stand behind the chaise lounge. "I thought you were going to teach me to swim," she said with forced lightness, "not dig out all my deep dark secrets."

"I haven't forgotten." His eyes swept the length of her, noting the renewed tension. "But first you have to relax. Otherwise you'll sink like a stone."

She glanced down at him furtively. "I am relaxed."

An arched eyebrow expressed his reservation. "If you keep this up, I'm going to start thinking you don't trust me."

Did she? The truth was, she wasn't certain. "I trust you enough to know you won't let me drown," she said, looking away from his dark, probing eyes and out at the colorful array of white, fuchsia and deep pink begonias ringing the grounds beyond the pool area. The fresh fragrance of late-summer flowers mingled with the scents of fruity suntan lotion and chlorinated water. It was an intoxicating combination. "I don't know how to swim, and I need to learn." Her glance returned to Nick and held, and she lifted one smooth shoulder. "You're willing to teach me."

"Not the greatest endorsement I've ever received," he said philosophically. He stood and placed the bottle of sunscreen on the nearby table.

"I'm sorry. That sounds ungrateful. And I do appreciate what you've done. Especially for Jason." After a moment, she added, "You've helped him to enjoy himself. That's very important to me."

"The voice of experience?"

She hesitated. "As you may have guessed, growing up I wasn't allowed to enjoy much of anything."

Nick heard a deep longing in her simple statement and experienced an immediate and unsettling need to satisfy it. What had started out as a means to ease his way into her life seemed to be turning into a desire to introduce her to all the experiences he was discovering she'd been denied. *Not smart, Saxon.*

Stephanie became aware of a new tautness in Nick. She cocked her head to one side. "What makes you think you *can* teach me to swim?"

A wicked smile spread across his strong features, replacing the momentary strain. "Because I'm an expert at difficult tasks."

His response was so unexpected, Stephanie threw her head back and laughed. "Great," she exclaimed, lifting her eyes skyward in mock despair. "He thinks of me as difficult."

"Take it as a compliment." He liked her sense of humor. When she laughed, her head thrown back and withholding nothing, she was the sexiest woman he'd ever met. From nowhere another thought leapt into his mind: Would she bring the same passion to lovemaking as well? The erotic image slammed into him.

Nick stripped off his knit shirt, then went to work on the buttons of his fly. "I told you earlier, I like challenges."

Stephanie watched every movement of his strong hands—the same hands that only moments ago had touched her skin with the same deftness. Her stomach fluttered at the provocative memory.

His body was beautiful—powerful, sculpted with hard muscle. She'd seen Nick in a swimsuit many times over the last few weeks and it hadn't affected her as it did right now. But today was different. Today she was alone with him, with no seven-year-old child to distract. Or protect. His civilized veneer seemed to have dropped away, leaving primitive male in its place. She felt the sensual kick all the way to her toes.

The only imperfection on his body was an ugly scar on his left shoulder that the deep bronzed color didn't quite conceal. He appeared unselfconscious about it. Or maybe he figured because it was so faint, no one would notice. And maybe she wouldn't have, Stephanie conceded, if she wasn't shamelessly examining every exposed inch of him.

She couldn't help wondering who had inflicted the scar—and what pain Nick must have endured. The urge to touch it and in some manner ease his past suffering was difficult for her to contain.

Nick's gaze collided with hers, and his eyes narrowed. He was painfully aware that her open scrutiny was having a very uncontrollable—and obvious—effect on the lower half of his body. He paused before shedding the last piece of clothing, wondering if she was prepared to witness what she did to him physically. Normally he wouldn't have hesitated. The women he usually dated were sophisticated enough to appreciate the prelude to sex. But even though she was thirty-eight years old and a mother, Stephanie possessed an intriguing innocence.

And it turned him on in ways that staggered him, considering his jaded attitude toward sex.

Keep your mind on business, Saxon. She's not here for sex. His brain might issue the order, he thought wryly, but his body wasn't listening.

Which left him with a problem. He cast a quick glance in Stephanie's direction, then turned his back to her. In one smooth motion he shucked off his jeans and took a running dive into the clear, cold water. He swam the entire length of the pool underwater. Twice. It was a tribute to years of harsh training and his rigid self-control. Only the need for oxygen finally forced him to the surface.

"Ready?" Nick asked as he swam to the side of the pool. By then the water had achieved the desired effect on the decidedly carnal part of his anatomy.

"As I'll ever be, I suppose." Now that the time had arrived to actually start the lesson, Stephanie had to struggle with her rising panic.

Nick got out of the water and walked over to her. Her expression was unguarded, her emotions exposed. And he didn't like the fear clearly etched on her features. "If it bothers you this much, you don't have to do it," he told her gently.

She squared her shoulders.

"Yes, I do."

"Tell me why you're so afraid."

"Oh, I don't know—something about not being able to breathe in that medium." Her shaky laugh didn't ring true.

Nick watched her, his steady gaze asking louder than words for an explanation.

Golden green eyes focused on his. "When I was very young I fell into a pond while on a field trip with my class." She laughed, but it sounded strained. "It scared the school officials more than it did me, I think. But my parents decided I shouldn't be allowed to take swimming lessons." She took a deep breath before continuing. "When I was about nine, I watched one of my classmates drown."

"While you were away at school." His rough-edged tone punctuated the statement.

She nodded slowly, no longer looking at him.

Nick muttered an oath. He had no trouble imagining how traumatic that had been to a child miles away from her family.

"It terrified me. But ridiculous as it might seem, I've always felt that if I'd known how to swim—" she inhaled sharply "—I might have been able to save her. But they wouldn't reconsider letting me take lessons. In fact, after that I wasn't allowed near a body of water larger than a bathtub."

Fury at whoever had made such an asinine decision mixed with empathy for a young girl who, at such a tender age, had blamed herself for her friend's death. Keeping the anger from his voice was difficult. "You'd think the school officials would've wanted all their students to know how to swim."

"My parents could be very persuasive. I'm sure they were trying to keep me safe." She turned to face him again. "So you see, it's past time I learned."

Nick detected the resolve in the stubborn set of her delicate jaw. "Okay," he said, "let's do it." Without thinking, he took her arm in a silent gesture of support and encouragement. He knew about fear and the desperation to conquer it. And he knew from personal experience how the touch of another human being could act as a lifeline in the blackness of terror.

She gingerly entered the water, and Nick felt the slight shudders that ran through her. He tightened his grip on her arm. "I won't let anything happen to you," he promised her.

"Thanks." The water was shockingly cold after the heat of the concrete apron, and Stephanie clenched her teeth to keep them from chattering. She concentrated on the hand that gripped her left arm like a gentle vise, not questioning why she found the strength contained there immeasurably reassuring.

Once they were waist deep, Nick turned her to face him. "Now comes the hard part."

Her eyes, almost black with apprehension, sought his. "Which is?" she asked, trying to inject some humor into her voice.

"I want you to lie on your back." Feeling another shudder rack her, he took hold of her other arm. "Don't worry. I won't let go of you. Will you trust me?"

His hands remained warm and comforting against the chill of the pool, Stephanie noted gratefully. The calluses had softened somewhat in the water, and she wondered absently where he'd gotten them. She scrutinized his face. What she saw written there was infinite understanding, as if he, too, had experienced terror and could empathize. Finally she closed her eyes and nodded.

Nick placed one arm around her shoulders, slipping the other under her knees and lifting her. "We're going to move a little farther out now. But not so deep that you can't put your feet down. Okay?" She nodded, and for timeless seconds he held her securely as he inched his way into deeper water. Without releasing her for a moment, he carefully positioned her so that she was floating. Instinctively, she grabbed for him.

"Easy, honey," he said, "I've got you." He watched as, by sheer willpower, Stephanie forced herself to submit her safety into his care. The simple act of faith did funny things to him.

The loose support of Nick's arms beneath her back and legs provided a sense of security, and almost without realizing it Stephanie slowly relaxed as she brought the fear under control. She became aware of her arm brushing against his chest—a very masculine, hair-roughened chest. The gentle pressure of his hand resting against her rib cage penetrated her consciousness, and a whole new set of sensations assailed her.

Nick had been torturously aware for some time that all he had to do was move just a few scant millimeters and his hand would envelop her breast. God, he'd been reduced to trying to cop a feel from a woman he was trying to teach to swim. A very *scared* woman. Though she'd relaxed somewhat since they'd entered the water, he wondered what her response would be if she picked up on the thoughts raging in his brain at the moment.

The strength of his sexual désire for this woman surprised him. Her body seemed to speak to him on some subliminal level that kept him off balance and... aroused. Even the cold water wasn't having a deterring effect any longer. Damn it, she wasn't the type of woman that usually created rampaging lust in him. Of course, he tried to rationalize, it had been a while since he'd last satisfied his natural urges. But his reaction to Stephanie told him he was definitely in worse shape than he'd realized.

"Ready for something a little more adventurous?"

She smiled languidly, feeling suspended in a silky medium that lapped gently against her in slow, lazy movements. "What else do you have in mind?"

"Questions like that can get you in a lot of trouble," he commented dryly.

"Trouble?" Stephanie repeated, opening her eyes to look up at Nick. He'd moved them into even deeper water, she realized, and his face was now disturbingly close—so close that she felt the warmth of his breath on the sensitive skin just above her breasts. But his head was silhouetted against the noonday sun, blocking out its brilliant rays. She sensed more than saw the intensity in his eyes. The water that only a short while ago had seemed incredibly cold did little to cool the heat being generated inside her.

"Never mind." Pursuing that course wasn't wise, he warned himself. "Are you game?"

"Well, so far it hasn't been too bad."

"If you keep giving me these extravagant endorsements, I'm sure to get a swelled head."

She chuckled. The sound was a bit wobbly, true, but it held genuine amusement.

Her growing confidence gave Nick a surprising amount of satisfaction. "I haven't failed you yet, have I?" It was almost more a question to himself than to her.

She continued to study his face, though his features remained shadowed. "No, you haven't." She smiled again. "So what's next, Teacher?"

From nowhere came the realization that Stephanie was beginning to trust him. But Nick's momentary elation was quickly replaced by concern. She didn't know who he really was or why he'd come to be in her life. She had a right to the whole story. And he had an obligation to tell her. In the beginning he'd rationalized that the truth might make her defensive, scare her off, perhaps cause her to see him as a threat to her and her son and their relationship.

Was that excuse still valid? The longer he waited, the more he betrayed Stephanie's faith in him and jeopardized her burgeoning trust. From what she'd told him about her life, he realized she wouldn't look kindly on him withholding this from her.

But he couldn't risk it. Not yet.

He had no choice but to wait for the right time. He'd tell her later, he silently swore, when they'd gotten to know each other better. He should walk away right now before things became any more complicated. But he couldn't, not without Jason.

He'd just have to make damned certain she never had cause to regret placing her trust in him.

Chapter Six

"I knew you'd be a fast learner," Nick said some time later as they hefted themselves onto the concrete edge of the pool.

"You're an excellent teacher." Invigorated by her accomplishment, Stephanie laughed through chattering teeth. The water had left her chilled even in the August heat, and she quickly burrowed through her carryall for a towel. Wrapping the thick turquoise-and-black terry cloth around her shoulders, she sat on the pool apron, allowing her shivering body to soak up the warmth trapped in the rust red bricks.

Nick dropped down next to her. He rested tanned forearms on his bent knees and looked at her. "Another of my many hidden talents."

She took note of the self-mocking amusement lurking in his dark eyes. "Now I understand why Jason is so eager to work with you. You're extremely patient."

"Comes naturally with a receptive student." His expression lost some of its teasing quality. "I can certify you're no longer in danger of drowning."

Her smile faded. "That's good to know."

"I've worked with some men who don't have the guts you do."

His compliment pleased her as few could. "I owe you one. Several, in fact." Today she'd conquered an old fear and learned something that made her feel just a little less different, a little more in step with the rest of the world. "Thank you."

"You're welcome." Her pleasure sparkled in her eyes, turning them a shimmering golden green. Watching her, Nick discovered, gave him a sense of satisfaction usually reserved for those moments after the successful wrap-up of a difficult intelligence operation.

Such a basic thing, learning to swim. But she seemed to revel in it. All she'd needed was a friend, someone whom she trusted and who was willing to show her a little patience and understanding. And increasingly, he found himself wanting to be just that—a friend. Not since Sally had the impulse been so strong.

Since his stint in Vietnam, he'd been a loner. His time there had done something to him that neither Sally nor his large, boisterous family could repair. But something about Stephanie got under his skin, touching a part of him that had been unreachable for years.

He pushed the unsettling realization away. "You could test your new skill by going sailing with me," he suggested quietly.

Stephanie detected another subtle dare. She pulled the towel tighter around herself. "Why a sailboat?"

"You mean, rather than a powerboat?"

She nodded.

"It's great for building shoulder muscles, something every serious swimmer needs. And learning to sail will give Jason another outlet for his competitive nature. There's nothing quite as satisfying as a man testing himself against the sea."

A frown marred her smooth forehead. "I want Jason to swim."

"That's natural," Nick said, "considering your experience with what can happen if you don't know how."

Stephanie nodded. "I just hadn't anticipated him becoming so obsessed with it."

"Some people might call it dedication." He felt a need to chase away Stephanie's troubled expression. "Look, all he needs is to learn that winning's not the most important thing in this life. Jason's a well-balanced kid. I think you worry too much."

His reassurance kindled a warm glow in Stephanie's heart. But she knew that what troubled Jason wasn't as simple as Nick might believe. "Is this another of your many talents, Mr. Saxon? Making worried mothers feel better?"

Something stirred deep within Nick. If there had to have been a mistake made, he was damned fortunate it was Stephanie who had become the mother of his child. The knowledge triggered a primal possessiveness in him. And an overpowering urge to share this with her. But he ruthlessly reined it in.

He couldn't afford to lose sight of his number-one priority. He had no way of knowing how Stephanie would respond to the news that he was Jason's father. First he had to establish a bond with Jason so strong it could withstand whatever battles might lie ahead. Perhaps a bond strong enough that it would discourage Stephanie from initiating any legal action against him, once she learned the extent of his deceit. He'd researched this area of the law and had found it sketchy at best. Definitive precedents a man in his position could rely on were almost nonexistent. He and Jason had grown close over the last several weeks, but not close enough for Nick to feel secure. No, he couldn't tip his hand.

But he was finding it harder and harder not to.

He forced a chuckle. "Something tells me Jason probably gets any 'obsessive' tendencies naturally."

A stricken look crossed Stephanie's features. "Why do you say that?"

"After this morning, I'd hazard a guess that you must have been a competitive little thing while growing up."

"Actually, the only person around to compete with was myself," Stephanie said evenly, remembering the loneliness. Then she changed the subject. "How did you get into the sideline of teaching kids, not to mention their mothers, to swim?"

Nick squinted out at the vibrant display of flowers several yards away. "I guess it's a good use of one of the few positive things that came out of my stint with the SEALs."

Stephanie heard the trace of bitterness in his voice. "Were you in Vietnam?"

He picked up a leaf that had fallen from one of the many trees on the densely wooded area close to the house, concentrating on it. "Yeah."

"Long?"

He rolled his shoulders as if trying to dislodge a heavy weight. "Long enough."

Stephanie searched for neutral ground. "What do Navy SEALs do?"

Shuttered now, his eyes cut to hers. His time in the military was something he didn't much care to talk about. "Do you get turned on by gruesome war stories?" he asked in a low voice.

The crude question stung, but she held his censuring stare and forced herself not to blink. "I'm not sure. Why don't you tell me one and I'll let you know?"

He'd underestimated her spunk, Nick realized. "Sorry. That was out of line." The question had been a self-protective reflex. Before it left his mouth he'd known it wasn't appropriate. But he'd run into his share of women circulating through the Washington social set who seemed to get a thrill out of hearing gory details.

The rigid set of his shoulders told Stephanie there was something here he didn't want to discuss. Apparently he had secrets, too. So why, she wondered, didn't she let the subject drop? "If you'd rather not talk about it..."

He was silent for several long moments, so long that she decided he would make no further comment. When he finally spoke, his voice held a rusty edge.

"Before the navy labels a man a SEAL, he has to be an expert in martial arts and demolition, and he sure as hell can use every kind of firearm known to mankind. Becoming an excellent swimmer is one of the few... benign skills they teach us. But it's essential to staying alive.

"My specialty was dropping behind enemy lines to sabotage their supply routes." And he and his team had been deadly proficient in their work.

Stephanie visibly shuddered. "Sounds extremely dangerous."

Nick laughed mirthlessly, remembering the grisly outcome of that last mission. "You could say that. The military is very efficient at training its men."

Stephanie picked up the slightly disparaging ring in his brief remark. "You should be proud of your service."

Proud? He thought of the casualty count from his expertise with explosives. Or from the Stoner Mark 23 machine gun he'd carried throughout his tour. The knowledge still had the power to give him a sick feeling in his gut. And the old nightmare still came back to torment him when he least expected it. "Wrong term, I think."

"What you did helped shorten the war and save lives."

Nick was unprepared for her simple acceptance. "There were a lot of people who didn't see it that way." Sally had said she understood. At least until she'd learned what his ultimate sacrifice to the war effort had been.

"Well, you did your job and came back safe and whole," she said.

"That's debatable," Nick said, not quite disguising the bleakness he felt. Safe and whole, if he didn't count losing something infinitely precious—the ability to create life. But, unaccountably, her words transformed an intolerable ache he'd carried for years into something almost bearable. Inexplicably, Stephanie made him feel a little cleaner, a little more complete than he'd felt in he couldn't remember how long.

"To answer your original question, working with kids was good therapy after I got home. After a while, I discovered I enjoyed it." Nick shrugged and tossed the leaf aside. "So," he said, steering the conversation back to his earlier request, and his thoughts away from this new and dangerous direction, "are you willing to try your luck on the boat?"

He'd closed the door, Stephanie knew immediately, on the subject of his military service. "If you think it will help Jason," she said, smiling slightly. "He needs a masculine influence in his life right now, so I'll bow to your judgment."

Nick studied Stephanie's delicate profile. "No male relatives?" he asked carefully.

Stephanie shook her head. "My parents died several years ago, and there's not much left of our family. No uncles or male cousins."

"No men in your life?"

"Men?"

"As in dates, boyfriends...lovers?"

Stephanie looked up to find him watching her with those dark, assessing eyes that seemed to delve into her. She felt a small electric current sizzle through her. Distractedly, she rubbed her arms. "I'm afraid my work schedule keeps me too busy for much of a social life."

She hadn't told him anything Nick hadn't already discovered for himself. Still, it gave him a surprising amount of satisfaction to hear her confirm it.

"Not that an active social life would make much difference," she continued. "I've always been cautious who I allow around Jason."

"Being too protective of a child can have its drawbacks."

Stephanie bristled at the gentle warning. She met Nick's eyes squarely. "That may be. But Jason is the most important thing in my life. At one time I wasn't certain I'd ever have a child. In my book there's no such thing as being too protective where he's concerned."

"Then I guess I should be flattered to be one of the chosen few." It was an attempt to lighten the mood. As he'd begun to suspect with a sense of foreboding,

Stephanie and Jason's relationship went deeper than that of most mothers and sons.

"As you've been quick to point out," Stephanie remarked dryly, "you have impeccable credentials."

And Nick had no doubt that she wouldn't be here otherwise. "What about his father?" He asked the question casually, as if it were a topic that could be discussed lightly.

Stephanie's breath seized in her chest. "I beg your pardon?"

"What about Jason's father?" he repeated evenly.

She looked at him sharply. "What about him?"

Nick shrugged lazily. Almost. Even in her own agitation over the unexpected question, Stephanie detected a renewed tension in him. There was no outward physical change. It was an intangible radiating of leashed energy. To a casual observer, Nick Saxon was simply relaxing in the sun, carrying on a friendly conversation. That she'd become so attuned to this man to pick up on something this subtle served to increase her agitation.

"It seems strange that I haven't heard him mentioned in the weeks I've spent with you and Jason."

A feeling of panic stole over her. The subject of Jason's father was one she'd never allowed herself to dwell on. At best it had the power to stir a gnawing ambivalence within her. She'd had to accept the fact that Jason would never know his father. But now a new thought had begun to niggle at the back of her mind. Would Jason's father approve of the way she was raising his son?

She stood quickly and began collecting her things. "There's nothing to mention."

"No?"

What would he say, she wondered, if she admitted the truth? If she simply came out and told Nick that she had no way of knowing who Jason's father was, even if she wanted to? That she'd wanted a child so desperately she'd chosen to conceive one by artificial insemination rather than risk the possibility of never having a child of her own? Because even eight years ago, there had been no man in her life.

But she wouldn't. She'd spent too many years protecting Jason and even longer guarding her own vulnerable emotions to be quite that open with this man who had thrust himself into her life only a few short weeks ago.

"There are no men in my life at the moment," she said with finality. "That includes Jason's . . . father."

For a split second Nick debated whether to push her further, then decided he was wiser to back off. He'd introduced the subject. Smart strategy dictated he give her time to think about it.

He rolled to his feet and walked over to her, stopping within touching distance. "Whatever you say."

Stephanie could feel the heat of him behind her. After stuffing everything into her carryall, she squared her shoulders and pivoted to face him. "Sorry." Her smile was brighter than warranted. "I'm not usually so defensive."

"Sometimes it helps to get things off your chest now and then," he suggested quietly. He watched her shoulders stiffen. "Don't ever apologize for being yourself, Stephanie," he said. "Particularly to me."

He made her feel oddly vulnerable. She hurriedly picked up her jumpsuit and slipped it on.

Nick wanted to ask Stephanie more. He wanted to know every tiny detail surrounding her decision to have

Jason. But he sensed she was struggling with a wound she kept so well-concealed he was certain few even knew it existed. The urge to pull her against him and simply hold her startled him. Without resisting the impulse, he lightly ran the fingers of his right hand down her bare arm. "You thirsty?" he asked huskily, hoping to ease the strain that had sprung up between them.

At his touch, Stephanie's gaze rushed to his. He was so close he seemed to eclipse everything else around her. He was squinting against the intense midday sun, but she detected the glitter in his dark-as-midnight eyes and again sensed the leashed energy radiating from him. But this energy was not the same as before. This was more potent. Something electric hummed between them, and for a heartbeat his hand tightened on her arm. Then he abruptly released her and stepped back.

Touching her again had been a mistake. They'd opened up too many secrets this morning, created a sense of intimacy without comprehending its full impact. Hell, in the state he was in, just being close to her was a mistake. He grabbed his shirt and shrugged into it. "Let's get out of this heat."

Nick's tone had become curt, and the guiding hand on Stephanie's elbow was impersonal. Without speaking, she followed his lead, allowing him to escort her up the flagstone steps and into the refreshing coolness of the kitchen. With quick, concise movements, he set out the ingredients for a light lunch. They ate in silence, the tension so thick it precluded conversation.

Stephanie finally excused herself and retrieved her things from the patio, where she'd left them earlier. In the powder room, where she retreated to regain her composure, she was amazed at the flushed cheeks and dilated eyes that stared back at her from the mirror. She splashed cool water on her face and went in search of Nick.

She found him still in the kitchen. He'd pulled on his jeans, she noted, but hadn't bothered to tuck in his shirt or put on shoes. The fact that he was standing in front of the sink, his hands submerged in soapy water, didn't begin to detract from the man's stark masculinity. He appeared endearingly domestic.

He glanced over his shoulder at her, his gaze speculative. "Tell me what it's like to be a genius."

Except for Alex, Stephanie had never in her thirty-eight years revealed personal details about herself to anyone. Particularly to a man—and one she didn't know all that well. She crossed her arms under her breasts, unconsciously warding off the invasion. This man probably had his pick of beautiful women. So why would he care about, or even be interested in, someone like her? And why was she even considering satisfying his curiosity? "Very boring topic, I can assure you."

"Somehow I doubt that." He looked over his shoulder at her again. "Talk to me."

She tensed slightly at his soft order. Maybe the heat of the morning sun, she mused, had bewitched her into complying. Or maybe it was the intensity of his gaze that seemed to envelop and mesmerize. She found herself capitulating almost against her will. "The best way to describe it is a feeling that your life isn't your own."

"In what way?" Nick prompted, when she didn't continue right away.

She moved over to the cherrywood table and began stacking, then restacking, the place mats into a neat pile of two. "Everyone expects something from you... starting as soon as your 'gift' is discovered."

"Surely your parents protected you?"

Stephanie considered her answer carefully. "To a degree. But they had their own expectations."

"Such as?"

"It was made very clear to me at a very early age that I was to learn as much as possible and that I was expected to use that knowledge."

And she'd spent her childhood trying to please them, Nick added silently. "Then the professional world must appreciate you."

"Depends on your definition of *appreciate*." Stephanie turned his words over in her head for several seconds. "It gets a bit tiresome being used to advance someone else's ambition."

"It never occurred to me that being a genius might be a disadvantage."

She laughed wryly. "Don't misunderstand. I've been fortunate. But I want control of my life," she said flatly. "I want to decide what's best for me and my son without someone telling me that I have other, more-important obligations. Or telling me how fortunate I am to be blessed with my intelligence."

Abandoning her self-imposed chore of meticulously aligning the place mats, Stephanie went to stand beside Nick at the counter. She picked up a towel and began drying the small number of dishes he'd placed on the drainboard. "I would cheerfully trade being super-smart for a better understanding of human nature." She'd always felt that her IQ had effectively separated her from mainstream society and every other normal person.

Her tone was light, but Nick heard the underlying loneliness. He didn't want to care that she'd been unhappy. But he did, and that scared him. Because he couldn't keep himself from wanting to do something about it. And he knew ultimately he would probably add to her pain.

He looked at her for several seconds. "There must be something positive about being a genius."

Sensing his questioning gaze, Stephanie smiled wryly. "It's great for discouraging would-be admirers."

Gently pulling the towel from Stephanie's fingers, Nick began drying his hands, all the while regarding her with interest. "And are there many?"

"Admirers?" she asked, wondering what to do with her now-empty hands.

One side of Nick's mouth tilted up slightly. "Yeah."

Except for colleagues, the dearth of men in her life was mortifying, if not downright humiliating. She had no intention of discussing that fact with Nick. Of course, she reminded herself, she'd already hinted at it on a couple of occasions. But she'd been trying to scare him off then, to protect Jason from disappointment. Or so she'd told herself. She mentally ran through several possible glib comebacks. "I've had my share."

Nick observed the slight blush tinting her cheeks. "Let me give you some good advice, Stephanie," he offered affably. "Don't lie. You're terrible at it."

Stephanie felt the heat in her face increase. "I suppose you're right." Her smile was rueful. "But a gentleman wouldn't mention it."

"Mention what? The fact that you don't lie well or that you don't have many male admirers?"

"Either. Both." When had he moved so close to her? she wondered, while fighting to control the flutter in her midsection. "Of course there are no admirers. You've known me a few weeks now," she reminded him. "Would you expect any?"

Nick groaned inwardly at her acceptance of just how unappealing she considered herself to men. It was hard to believe that she hadn't a clue just how impossibly tempting she was. Nor how dangerously close he was to giving her a graphic demonstration.

He braced his hands against the counter on either side of Stephanie. It effectively trapped her in the corner. "I'll give you another piece of advice."

He was so close that for the first time she could see silver flecks in his dark irises. "If it's anything like the last," she commented with self-mockery, "I'm not sure I'm ready for it."

Nick didn't share her amusement. Something flared in his eyes, but his expression remained impassive. "It's not wise to credit a man with qualities he doesn't deserve."

She searched his face, trying to decipher the warning in his words. "Is that what I'm doing?"

"Oh honey, are you ever."

Uncertainty replaced her earlier humor. "In what way?"

"Don't assume I'm a gentleman," he warned. The hot gaze he ran over each feature of her face could have melted lead. "Right at this moment there's nothing I'd like better than to show you how wrong you are."

She lifted her shoulders in puzzlement. "About what?"

A muscle rippled along his jaw. He hadn't realized such naiveté still existed in the world. It was having an disturbing effect on his self-control. "About how unappealing you think you are to the opposite sex. About your assumption that you don't tempt a man."

Oh, what the hell. He didn't question his motives. He simply eased his body against hers and lowered his head, keeping his hands firmly planted on the counter.

Nick's mouth hovered a breath away from Stephanie's for long heartbeats as he silently asked permission. Refusing him never entered her head. Like a magnet, the heat radiating from him drew her mouth the scant millimeter needed, bringing it into full contact with his. The initial stroke of her lips to his sent a kaleidoscope of sensations washing through her. She felt the rush of warm air against her cheek as his mouth settled more firmly over hers. He was incredibly gentle, she noted dimly, while in the same instant he demanded total participation from her.

And she didn't disappoint him. Nick heard a guttural sound and couldn't say whether it had come from Stephanie or from him. Angling his head, he tested the satiny seam of her mouth, and she willingly parted her lips to accommodate him. His tongue eagerly invaded her warmth, finding, then thoroughly exploring all the sensitive areas within. She tasted of the fruit they'd shared at lunch, mixed with an intoxicating tang that was as old as Eve. This time he knew the groan was his—and that he was in big trouble.

Nick smelled of chlorine and sunshine and musk, and Stephanie couldn't get enough. She pushed against him, unconsciously aligning her body closer to his. The feel of hard male muscle and bone in such intimate contact with her much-softer body added a whole new dimension to the sensations assaulting her. Her legs seemed to have lost their ability to support her, and she had no choice but to cling tighter to Nick.

Some tiny part of Stephanie questioned why she wasn't affronted by what he was doing. But she quickly silenced it. What he stirred in her was too powerful, too unique, and that part of her that had been denied all her life yearned for everything he was offering.

Hers wasn't the practiced kiss of the women Nick usually dated. It was tentative, with a subtle, innocent sensuality that spoke compellingly to some primal part of him. And she excited him, he now conceded, as no other woman ever had.

She was eager, he marveled, so eager that she was destroying his normal ironclad control. Wondering vaguely when he'd allowed himself to put his arms around her, he pulled her tighter, suddenly aware of her fragility—and her vulnerability. He'd intended to keep his hands firmly planted on the counter on either side of her. He'd intended simply to kiss her, to show her how desirable she was. He hadn't intended to lose control. The last thing he wanted was to frighten her.

Nick forced himself to lift his head and examine Stephanie's flushed face. She slowly opened her eyes, a sigh of protest escaping her. There was no longer even a trace of her earlier inhibitions, he noted. Her pupils were dilated to almost black, with only a thin band of golden green encircling them. They held a smoldering, slumberous quality, as if she'd just been awakened from a long sleep.

He wanted nothing more than to lay her back against the kitchen counter and make hot, sweet love to her. Instinctively, he ran his hands down her supple back, cupping her gently rounded fanny and drawing her lower body securely against his.

"Just as I imagined," he said, his voice guttural, "you're as quick at learning to kiss as you were at learning to swim." He rested his forehead against hers and tried to drag enough oxygen into his lungs. "God, honey, you're something else."

"Is that good or bad?" She realized it was a very weak attempt at humor.

"Good. Too damned good."

There was a slightly mocking note in his words, and the first niggling embarrassment penetrated Stephanie's sensual haze. "Can something be *too* good?"

The chime of the doorbell saved Nick from having to answer. He issued a one-word profanity that summed up his frustration exactly.

He felt Stephanie flinch, then withdraw. Not a physical withdrawal, because his body still held hers trapped in the corner of the counter. But her mental and emotional retreat was instantaneous and complete. He cursed again.

"What time is it?" Disoriented, she looked around for a clock. "That must be Alex. I told her to pick me up at two." She realized she was babbling, and bit her wayward tongue.

The doorbell sounded again, and Nick reluctantly released her and stepped back. "I'll get it." His gaze wandered down the length of her, then returned to study her flushed face and kiss-swollen lips. He didn't like leaving her like this, and would have cheerfully kept the untimely intruder waiting at his front door until the end of the next ice age. He expelled a harsh breath. But if it was indeed Alex, that would only cause more problems.

"You might want to freshen up," he suggested huskily.

She glanced at him gratefully. "Yes, I think I will," she said.

Nick watched her leave the room. The interruption couldn't have come at a worse time, he realized. He shoved the fingers of one hand through his hair and cursed again. Turning on his heels, he headed for the door.

Chapter Seven

"I was beginning to think I'd gotten the time wrong," Alex said neutrally as they drove away from Nick's house.

"Excuse me?" Stephanie pulled herself away from the thoughts swirling around in her head and looked at her sister sharply.

"Or maybe I just showed up at a bad time?"

Alex, Stephanie noted, didn't seem the least perturbed by her scowl. "No. We were..." She searched for a credible excuse. "I guess we just didn't hear the doorbell when you first rang it."

"Or the second, third or fourth time," Alex said blandly, returning her attention to the road.

"Sorry. We were... talking."

"Ah."

Stephanie took an immediate interest in the scenery passing in a blur outside the window on her side of the car. She hated it when her sister said "ah" in just that tone. It intimated that she didn't believe for a minute whatever she was telling her. And it was making Stephanie feel like a teenager who'd been caught necking.

Well, isn't that what you were doing? a tiny voice accused.

Yes, but she was a consenting adult, she argued. She could kiss a man if she wanted to. She didn't owe anyone an explanation.

And she'd definitely wanted to, Stephanie admitted candidly. Her stomach bottomed out at the erotic memories. Damn, she should be driving. That would have given her something else to concentrate on rather than what had taken place such a short time ago in his kitchen.

"How'd the lesson go?" Alex asked, her change of topic initiating a relieved inward sigh from Stephanie.

"It went . . . well."

Alex glanced at Stephanie. "Well?"

She nodded. "Nick tells me that I'm no longer in danger of drowning."

"That's good. And in just one lesson. Quite an accomplishment, considering your lack of enthusiasm for bodies of water larger than a mud puddle."

Several seconds of silence stretched between them. "He's very good at distracting a person."

"So you do find him interesting?"

Stephanie's gaze cut to her sister. "That's not what I said."

"Oh, come on, Sis. There's definitely something there when the two of you get anywhere near each other. The condition you were in when I picked you up wasn't caused by simply playing around in the pool all morning."

"Maybe," she conceded grudgingly.

"Well, hallelujah."

Stephanie rolled her eyes and resigned herself to Alex's grilling. The imprint of Nick's kiss still burned her mouth. She'd never been that...uninhibited with a man before. Of course, there hadn't been that many men before, either. She frowned slightly, wondering what had come over her.

"Hey, don't look so concerned. If it gets too complicated, you can always dump him."

"Or he could dump me." Then Stephanie added mildly, "I believe dumping men is *your* specialty. One you execute, I might add, with considerable flair."

Alex winced at the gentle reminder and chuckled. "Only those that fit into the Neanderthal category."

"I'm surprised you have no reservations about Nick."

"What can I say?" Alex lifted one shoulder, bare except for a tumble of honey blond hair and the tiny strap of her tank top. "He's good with kids. That says something for him."

"True." Jason was positively thriving under Nick's attention. "Still, there's something about him...." Stephaie let her words trail off.

"Stephie dear, you've got to stop mistrusting every person you meet, particularly men. Maybe it's fate."

"I don't believe in fate."

"Again speaks the scientist. Where's your sense of adventure?"

"It's been sufficiently put out of its misery."

"Well, let me put your mind at rest," Alex commented. "You might be interested in some of the things I found out about him."

Stephanie jerked her head around to stare at her. "You checked him out?"

"I have to look out for my big sister, don't I?"

Alex's words touched Stephanie. She and her sister were direct opposites in personality. Yet because of their unusual upbringing, they'd forged a deep love and friendship, and Stephanie tolerated from Alex what she never would from any other person.

Curiosity overcame her initial surprise. "And what did you find out?"

"He's well-off financially." Alex grinned and glanced at Stephanie. "So I doubt he's after your money."

"I figured that out for myself." Nick was far too independent and had too much pride for that. Instinctively she knew that he wouldn't want anything he hadn't earned. But what was his he'd claim without reservation.

"One thing's for sure, he's definitely not your average government operative. He circulates in the highest diplomatic circles, but keeps a very low profile."

Stephanie felt a ripple of unease. "Meaning?"

"No one seems to know exactly what he does. It's as if there's an invisible wall protecting him. What answers I did get—which were damned few—were always sketchy."

Stephanie took her time digesting this. Why was someone as important as Nick appeared to be bothering with an assignment as mundane as the one at the lab? If anyone could dig out facts about a person, it was Alex. Few people had the contacts that were accessible to her in police work. That she'd run into a dead end was puzzling. Well, Stephanie had always been good with puzzles. But something told her this one was a lot more intriguing than any she'd ever attempted to solve before. And probably a lot more dangerous.

"Maybe he's just a very private person," she finally said, shaking off the thought.

"That would certainly explain why he's never high profile, even at obligatory functions."

Stephanie had no trouble imaging that scenario. *Obligatory* wasn't a word she'd envision in Nick Saxon's vocabulary. She knew he'd do exactly what he chose. "Are you endorsing him or trying to warn me off?"

Alex grinned. "Just giving you the facts, ma'am. He also has the reputation of being a barracuda. Rumor has it that he's good to have at your back during a fight. On the flip side, I'd hate to have him for an enemy."

Stephanie readily agreed with that. Nick Saxon would be a force to reckon with—one she wasn't certain she'd be capable of handling.

Nothing she'd done seemed to discourage the man or turn him off. Again she felt the seductive pressure of his mouth on hers. Never had she experienced such overpowering sexual arousal. It had been as frightening as it had been stimulating.

Certainly her brief relationship with a teaching assistant at one of the many colleges she'd attended didn't compare. She had been younger than all her classmates, and she remembered feeling lost. Jim had seemed so eager to be her friend. They'd both been working on their Ph.D.s in physics. She'd thought they had a lot in common, but the experience had proved less than satisfying. In fact, ultimately it had proved degrading, particularly when she'd accidentally discovered that he was primarily interested in using her brains to further his own academic research.

That's when she'd begun to suspect that she wasn't like other women. A couple of other less-devastating, but disillusioning relationships had finally convinced her. God had given her too many brains and apparently not enough of the other qualities to attract, and hold, a man.

She wouldn't make the mistake, Stephanie told herself firmly, of taking Nick's apparent interest in her too seriously. All she had to do was keep in mind that this situation could never amount to anything permanent.

But a little exploration couldn't hurt, could it?

There was so much blood!

Three of his men were already down, and another injured. Screams rent the air—the screams of humans mixed with the higher-pitched, mechanical screams of mortar shells. Adrenaline surged through his system as one burst scant yards from him and his remaining men as they scrambled for safety.

Damn! They had to find cover or his entire squad was going to be wiped out. Cold sweat soaked his already wet camouflage fatigues and mingled with the blood oozing from his left shoulder.

"Smith! You and Carter get Jacobs into that ravine to your right!"

His shouted order was all but obliterated by the sound of another shell exploding at closer range, followed by the staccato rat-tat-tat of enemy gunfire. A flash of white caught the corner of his eye. Heart pounding, he jerked his machine gun into position, instantly ready to eliminate the potential threat. His finger started to squeeze the trigger, just as he saw Delaney spray the area with deadly 9-mm shells.

*The stench of gunpowder, dirt and decaying vegeta-
tion filled his nostrils, gagging him. The next incoming
shell flung him to the ground, at the same time illumi-
nating the area. When he regained his senses, two fig-
ures dressed in light-colored clothing lay motionless on
the ground. He saw Delaney start toward them in a
crouch, just as the smaller one struggled to his feet. This
time gut instinct and finely honed reflexes ordered him
to protect his man at all cost, and he pulled the trigger,
sending out a barrage of lethal fire.*

*A split second too late he registered that the now-still
form was that of a small boy.*

Nick jerked awake, a scream of denial still raging in
him. His body felt clammy, drenched in cold sweat, and
bile burned his throat. He sat up in the rumpled bed and
dragged shaking hands down his face, wondering if he'd
live long enough to escape the horror of this particular
nightmare.

He turned on the bedside lamp to banish the haunt-
ing night shadows, then swung his legs over the side of
the bed and headed for the liquor cabinet in his study.
Pouring himself some whiskey, he drank it down in one
swallow, choking as it burned its way to his belly.

But it couldn't erase the image of the child from his
mind.

He'd thought he'd gotten the nightmares under control. It had been a while since the last one. He walked
over to the study window. Rubbing the back of his
neck, he stared out at the darkened silhouette of the
trees out back, the echo of other, deadlier silhouettes
still vivid in his mind's eye. What had dredged this up
from his subconscious? he wondered.

Maybe it was his conversation earlier today with Stephanie.

Maybe it was the fact that his son was just about the same age as that boy in that nameless jungle village an eon ago.

Maybe it was because he'd just found something so infinitely precious to him that he was gut-deep scared of losing it.

He searched for something to dispel his grim thoughts. The image of Stephanie's kiss-swollen mouth floated to the surface, displacing the uglier images of war and death. One tension within him eased, while another of an entirely different nature replaced it. He could recall with aching clarity how sweetly abandoned her untutored response had been.

But then the memory of the stunned expression on her face took its place. Alex's interruption couldn't have come at a worse time. He cursed succinctly.

He shouldn't have allowed himself to take advantage of Stephanie, he thought. He might want her, but he knew better than to make a move on someone as unsophisticated as she was. Still, he couldn't suppress a moment of pure masculine satisfaction at having been able to arouse her.

Nick shook his head at his lapse in self-control. His purpose in offering to teach her to swim had been to show her that she had nothing to fear from him. His strategy had been to carefully steer her from discussion about her work into more intimate areas of her life. To glean answers to questions such as why had she never married? Why had a woman as sexy as she was chosen artificial insemination to conceive a child? And what had she told Jason about his absent father?

He certainly hadn't planned on seducing her—even if he'd been motivated to show her just how infinitely desirable she was.

Time was running out. At any moment Matt could call, telling Nick to drop everything and report at once. And he'd have to go. His partner was out there somewhere on his own. Slater had been more than willing to give Nick the precious time needed to handle his own personal crisis. Under no circumstances would he desert him.

Nick's work had been his salvation for so many years. After his wife's death, living on the edge had given him a sense of purpose. He'd never questioned his decision. Why shouldn't he take the risks and leave the safer assignments to those men who had families—who were fathers? Men who could become fathers?

He exhaled heavily and raked both hands through his hair. But now his priorities had changed radically; he was no longer interested in danger. He had something to live for, a legacy, a child. But Nick never, never left an assignment before it was finished. And deserting his partner was unthinkable. He might want to pull out of this one, but not while Slater might be in danger. There was no question that Nick was in this operation until it was finished.

He hoped that would be soon.

The shrill ring of the phone cut off his brooding thoughts. He picked it up hoping it was Slater. Nick hadn't heard from him in several days, which was unusual for his partner.

It was Matt. "We've got a problem. Can you get over here now?"

"On my way," Nick said, and hung up.

In his line of work, he was considered very efficient at damage control. He smiled bleakly into the darkness beyond his window.

He hoped to hell his reputation held—not only in his professional life, but his personal life as well.

The insistent peal of the doorbell halted Stephanie's quick progress up the stairs. Who would be calling on her at nine o'clock at night? The last thing she needed at the moment was a visitor; she had to get to the lab. She reversed directions and headed for the front door. Jerking it open, she was astonished to find Nick Saxon lounging against the doorjamb.

"Hi," he said without preamble.

"Hi yourself." She hadn't seen him in almost three days and found herself hungrily taking in every detail. His hands were shoved into the pants pockets of a dark, obviously expensive suit. He looked as if he'd come straight from a business meeting or some significant social function. She felt a moment's irritation at herself for wondering which—and if the latter, who he had been with.

In deference to the muggy August evening, he'd loosened his tie and unfastened several buttons of the pristine white dress shirt he wore. Stephanie sensed an almost indiscernible difference in him tonight. He seemed less accessible—and much more formidable.

"Doesn't this place have a security system?" His glance swept the secluded area surrounding the house.

"You know it does." He'd asked her about it shortly after he'd begun investigating the security problem at the lab. "Why do you ask?"

"Why isn't it on?"

"Alex and Jason left a short while ago," she explained, puzzled by his abrupt questions. "I haven't gotten around to resetting it yet."

"Not wise, Dr. Harcourt. You never know who might wander up to your door." He straightened from his relaxed stance, withdrawing one hand from his pocket. "You forgot this." He picked up her carryall and held it out to her. "I thought you might need it."

"Oh." Remembering the intimate circumstances preceding her hasty departure the last time they'd been together, Stephanie felt color sweep up her cheeks. "You didn't need to go out of your way to return it."

He watched her steadily. "Yes, I did."

Stephanie took the tote from his outstretched hand. "Thank you."

"You're welcome." He waited a beat, then smiled crookedly. "I like your glasses."

Stephanie automatically reached to remove them. "Thanks." She'd forgotten she had them on. She rarely wore them. Some repressed vestige of vanity, she supposed, had forced her into contacts several years ago. But when her eyes became tired, like tonight, she reverted to eyeglasses.

"I realize it's late, but do you mind if I come in?"

"Oh. Of course not," she said, stuffing her glasses into one pocket of her shorts. "Come in."

Nick stepped into the lighted entrance hall, closing the door behind him and leaning against it.

His gaze trailed a path from her bare feet upward, until reaching her eyes. "Are you all right?"

"All right?" Stephanie echoed, thinking that should be *her* question. He looked exhausted, the lines in his face accentuated by a subtle tension in him.

Something flashed in his eyes, then was shuttered. "I won't apologize for kissing you," he said, frustration edging his voice.

"I don't expect you to." Stephanie was pleased that her voice was cool, that she sounded in control. She'd intended to try and act blasé and sophisticated about the whole incident the next time she saw him. But she hadn't expected to see him looking so tired. Or so vulnerable.

"You responded," he continued as if she hadn't spoken, pushing the fingers of one hand through his hair. "You put as much into it as I did."

It was almost an accusation, Stephanie decided. "Look, Nick, can we hold the postmortems until later? I've got to get to the lab." She was suddenly grateful for the unavoidable errand that had been interrupted by Nick's sudden arrival.

"This late?" He glanced at the black diver's watch on his left wrist, then more sharply back at her.

"I don't have a choice. Someone just called to tell me that one of the computers crashed. I need to reload the program."

"Yours?"

"No. This is for a colleague."

He looked surprised. "Don't they have backup files?"

"Yes. But I wrote the program and the backups stay with me. No one else is allowed to touch them."

Absently he massaged his neck. "Mind if I tag along?" He'd dropped by to determine what damage his reckless kiss of a few days ago had done. He'd have been here the next day if not for complications on his current assignment. Now he didn't intend to leave until he found out what was going on in her mind—and then he'd only depart after he'd done whatever was necessary to repair any damage.

He refused to acknowledge the fact that he'd also had a powerful need to see her.

"Why?" she asked in bewilderment, looking at him sharply. "Do you think this has something to do with the security breaches?"

"It wouldn't hurt to check it out," Nick said noncommittally. His stomach rumbled just then, loud enough for Stephanie to notice. He grimaced apologetically. "I didn't have time for lunch. Or dinner. Maybe we could grab a bite after you're finished."

"This may take awhile," she felt obligated to warn him.

"I promise I'll find some way to entertain myself. And I think I can restrain myself from eating the furniture." Nick held her gaze for several long heartbeats. "I'd like some company right now," he added quietly.

The soft admission was the last thing she would've expected from him. She was finding his strange mood disconcerting, accustomed as she was to his usual tight control. "Fine. Make yourself at home," she said as she started for the stairs. "I'll be right down."

After she'd left the room, Nick looked around the spacious living area. This was the first time he'd been inside her home. He wandered over to the entertainment center and studied the collection of CDs. The eclectic selection seemed almost incongruous with the rather formal, stilted tenor of the house.

One long wall of the room was covered with bookshelves, and he sauntered over to examine their contents. There was a large and varied selection of mysteries, science fiction, children's stories, romances, current bestsellers, interspersed with biographies and a wide range of classics.

But it was the children's books he kept returning to. There were hundreds of them, some quite old, some more recent. Most intriguing was a small group of these books, newer than those that had perhaps been Stephanie's when she was a child and separated from those that had probably been purchased for Jason. All were by the same author, one whose stories his nieces and nephews frequently cajoled him into reading to them.

Interesting, Nick thought. The house said one thing while Stephanie's personal possessions said something else entirely.

He explored a little longer, then dropped down onto the leather sofa. Letting his head rest against the cushiony back, he tried to stave off the fatigue caused by the recurring nightmare. And two days that had been really tough. All he needed was to rest his eyes for a couple of minutes.

Stephanie returned a short while later to find Nick slumped on the couch. The signs of strain etched on his face even in sleep touched something within her. He seemed to be suffering, and her need to ease it was surprisingly strong.

He came awake with a jerk, instantly alert, ready to take on some unknown enemy. Becoming aware of his surroundings, he propped his elbows on his widespread knees and rubbed his face. "Sorry. Must have dozed off."

"You look frazzled." The fatigue and shadow of pain she glimpsed in his eyes before he masked them generated in Stephanie the urge to put her arms around him. She'd sensed that touch of vulnerability.

He rubbed his face again. "Something came up at the agency."

"A problem?"

"You could say that."

She smiled sympathetically. "This must be the day for problems at work."

She'd changed into a pale blue dress of a comfortable-looking material that made him want to touch it to see if it were as soft as it appeared. "Where's Jason?" he asked, to distract his wayward thoughts.

"Alex took him to see a movie."

He nodded and his gaze swept the room. "You take care of this place all by yourself?"

Stephanie raised an eyebrow, wondering if he was teasing her for her comments of several days ago about his own home. "If you're referring to the cleaning arrangements, no. Mrs. Hobson and a staff of servants run it. This is their night off."

His mouth curved into that rare, beguiling grin that did dangerous things to her heart. "What I mean is, do you and Jason rattle around this place alone?"

"No. Alex lives here, too. At least most of the time." Stephanie picked up her car keys and a box of computer disks she'd brought downstairs with her. "Shall we take my car?"

"Good idea. I'm so tired I'd probably be a menace on the road." He followed her out to the four-car garage.

"Nice house, but it's not you," Nick commented as Stephanie negotiated the winding drive.

"Thanks." She glanced at him, then back to the road, absurdly pleased that he'd noticed. "I agree."

"Then why are you living here?"

"I guess because it represents the only constant in my childhood." She hesitated. "It's a link with my parents, with family tradition."

Nick heard the wistfulness in her voice. Tradition and permanence were important to her. So why had someone like her chosen artificial insemination to conceive her son?

Damn it, he wanted to be able to talk openly to Stephanie. He didn't like lying to her. He liked it less with each passing day. True, his was a lie of omission rather than commission, but it was a lie just the same. He leaned back against the headrest and closed his eyes. And yet he still felt he had to keep up the pretense, at least for a while longer.

Chapter Eight

The lab facility was located out in the Maryland countryside northeast of Washington. It was situated next to the gently rolling hills of an agricultural complex. Stephanie had always thought it incongruous for something containing such sophisticated technology to be juxtaposed against something so unpretentiously rural.

As they approached the security gate, she looked over at Nick. "Do you have your pass with you?"

"No," he said, not opening his eyes. "I hadn't planned on this little trip. But don't worry."

Raising a skeptical eyebrow, she fumbled for her own ID and handed it to the guard.

"Good to see you, Dr. Harcourt," the guard said, handing it back. He bent down to look through the window at Nick, still slouched in the passenger seat. "And you, sir?"

Nick removed an official-looking card from his wallet and handed it across to the guard. The motion was so smooth and discreet that Stephanie had no opportunity to get a good look at it, much less read what was written on it. The guard gave it a quick glance and just as discreetly handed it back to Nick. They were admitted without further questions.

"How'd you do that?" she asked as she proceeded through the gate to the reserved-parking area behind the smaller building that housed Stephanie's lab.

Nick shrugged and smiled crookedly, making Stephanie's heart do a crazy little dance. "I keep telling you I have good references."

"One of these days," she said dryly, stepping out of the car, "I'm going to demand to see a complete list of those references."

"Maybe we could negotiate something."

"Like what?" she asked, eyeing him dubiously.

"I'll tell you a deep dark secret if you'll tell me one."

She shot him a look expressing her reservations. In her relatively short time with him she'd learned that he didn't like giving away secrets about himself any more than she did.

They entered the building, and Stephanie led the way to the door at the end of a long corridor. When she inserted her security card, the door opened into her strictly utilitarian office, crowded with numerous computers printing out reams of data. A more-sophisticated computer, its screen blank, sat off to one side of the large room. Stephanie headed over to it and sat down.

"You can reprogram someone else's computer from this office?" Nick asked when she opened the box she'd brought with her and began extracting diskettes.

Stephanie looked up as she fed one into the disk drive. "Yes. I can access all the computers in the lab from mine."

"Why?"

"Since I wrote so many of the programs used here, it seemed logical to set it up this way."

"Very convenient."

"Is that significant?"

He shrugged. "Any piece of information is significant in an investigation."

"I see," she said absently, concentrating on her task.

He walked over to a desk situated in front of the only window in the room, within a few feet of where she now sat. As always, the surface was cluttered with printouts, scientific books and magazines and other miscellaneous things. But for the photograph of Jason, her desk contained nothing personal, nothing that would make it a pleasant place to spend the countless hours Nick was certain were demanded in Stephanie's line of work.

"How do you choose among all the projects you're offered?"

Stephanie paused in the process of inserting the next disk. For a moment she looked perplexed. "I've never really thought about it."

"Do you take the highest offer?"

Stephanie frowned. "I don't think so. I certainly don't need the money."

"Then is it because you love one project more than another? Or find one more exciting?"

Before answering, Stephanie finished inserting the disk and pressed Enter. "Not really."

He looked around the nondescript room. "Then why do you do any of this?"

She considered his question while she ejected the disk and inserted another. There it was again—another foray into her personal life. Stephanie recalled Alex's account of what she'd uncovered about Nick Saxon. Or rather what she couldn't. He might have good references and credentials, but what did Stephanie really know about him?

She mentally shook her head. Lord, she was fast on her way to becoming paranoid. So far Nick had given her no reason to distrust him—either professionally or personally. She was being very unfair to a man who'd gone out of his way to be nice to her son. And her.

She finally realized that Nick was still waiting for an answer. "Because I'm supposed to."

"Supposed to?" He studied her profile. "Says who?"

Stephanie smiled wryly. "Professors, mentors, colleagues." After a moment she added quietly, "When they were alive, my parents."

"And what do *you* want?" Nick asked, strolling over to stand next to her chair.

No one as far back as she could remember had ever asked her that question. What *did* she want? "To be accepted like anyone else. To be allowed to pursue the same things that others can without question. To have control of my life."

"You don't enjoy your work?"

"That's not what I mean. I like the concept of space exploration better than most projects I've been offered." She lifted one shoulder. "But this is probably not the most productive thing I could possibly do."

"I disagree. It's very productive. It opens new frontiers for mankind to conquer. It's a great fantasy."

That surprised her. He'd tapped into what had kept her going for so many years. The fantasy of escape, of determining one's own destiny.

He waited while she removed another disk and inserted the next, then he swiveled her chair to face him, propping his hands on its arms, effectively trapping her. "What other fantasies do you have, Stephanie?"

Her heart skittered, as much from the intensity radiating from Nick as from the closeness of his body to hers. She was acutely conscious of him as a man tonight. There seemed to be a direct correlation, she was discovering, between his probing gaze and the odd melting sensation taking place deep within her.

"Is this one of those questions that's negotiable?" Stephanie swallowed to ease the huskiness in her voice that hadn't been present moments ago.

One side of Nick's mouth lifted, but with minimal humor. "Give me a fantasy that will wipe out the last thirty-six hours and you've got a deal."

The weariness in his words wrenched at Stephanie's heart. "Sounds fair enough."

Her computer *bleeped*, reminding them of why she was here. Nick slowly straightened away from her, and she released a tightly held breath. She focused on the task at hand, fighting to regain her composure. After several minutes, she swiveled again to face him.

"A fantasy..." Her brow furrowed in concentration. "How's this? Once upon a time there was a great warrior, fearless and powerful, who lived in a troubled land. He felt it his duty to rescue those in peril and avenge terrible wrongs. Then one day he found he was in need of help. And those that he'd helped in the past wanted to return the favor."

Nick leaned against one corner of her desk, listening with interest.

"But he refused their offers," she continued, "because he had a reputation of being invincible and believed he had to live up to it. Pretty soon, the people began to fear him, and instead of seeking his help, they fled from him."

Momentary confusion flickered across his harsh features. "Why would they become afraid of him?"

"Because when the warrior wouldn't tell them what troubled him, they began to speculate among themselves. And what they came up with was far worse than the truth."

He studied her for several long seconds, his features now unreadable. "Is there a princess in this story?"

"This is a fantasy," she said, struggling to keep her tone light. "There's always a princess."

"And she's very beautiful."

It wasn't really a question, but she took it as one. "Of course." She pursed her lips. "Aren't all princesses beautiful?"

"Outside, maybe. Not necessarily inside."

"But this is your fantasy. She can be any way you want."

Nick smiled wryly. "And what does she think of the warrior?"

"She thinks he's brave and noble, that the people simply don't understand him."

Nick raised an eyebrow. "Isn't that the line warriors are accused of using to string princesses along?"

"Ah, but it depends," Stephanie said sagely, "on the context in which it's used."

His dark eyes crinkled in amusement, and he shook his head. "Tell me—by any chance, is this warrior handsome?'' With his frame still propped against the desk, he crossed one ankle over the other.

Out of the corner of her eye, Stephanie followed the casual movement. On numerous occasions over the past few weeks she'd witnessed those powerful legs, bare of clothing, propel Nick through the water at championship speeds. She didn't remember them having quite the same effect on her as they were tonight. "Hmm." She cocked her head to one side, as if giving his question serious consideration. "Oh yes. Very."

"Does the warrior—" Nick reached out and lifted a silky strand of hair away from her cheek "—have any chance of sweeping the beautiful princess off her feet?"

Stephanie hadn't realized he'd moved within touching distance. Reflexively she adjusted her glasses. Never before had she thought of them as a shield, but tonight she was grateful for that one fragile barrier against Nick's potent masculinity. "Simply because he's handsome?"

He lifted one shoulder. "Whatever works."

Stephanie was beginning to feel she'd lost control of the situation. She ran her tongue over suddenly dry lips. "Is it that important to the warrior that he succeed?"

Nick's gaze followed the innocently provocative movement of her tongue before searching her upturned face, as if seeking some critical truth. "Tell me about the princess."

"She's very perceptive," she said, unable to break the intangible connection that seemed to draw her to him. "She senses his suffering."

"And what does she do about it?" There was the barest trace of cynical amusement in his tone.

"She listens while he talks."

"Ah, but the question is—" all banter vanished from his voice, his expression growing serious "—will she understand?"

"Is that what you want?"

Nick released the antique golden curl he'd been fondling and moved a short distance away, shoving his hands into the pockets of his slacks, his back to her. "What I want is something that will blot out hell. Something that will give me back my life."

Again the bone-deep weariness tinged his words. Stephanie doubted he was even aware he'd spoken aloud. It touched a chord within her. Something about the tension she sensed in Nick tonight made her want to reach out to him, ease whatever was bothering him. She left her chair and walked over to him, impulsively placing a hand on his broad shoulder. Through the fine fabric of his suit jacket she felt hard muscles flex. "Will you tell me what's wrong?"

"You don't want to know." His shoulders lifted on a harsh breath. It was ugly, and she didn't deserve to be contaminated.

"Nothing can be that bad."

He knew he shouldn't talk about it. And if he hadn't been so tired, he would never even consider it. But just this once, he needed to share the burden. *Yeah, and what are you going to tell her? That you're a murderer and a fraud in the bargain?* That should certainly put her mind at ease. He took a half step away, severing the physical contact, then turned to face her.

Oddly, the small act of rejection hurt. Stephanie could decipher nothing from his grim expression. Only the steady hum of computers and the clatter of printers filled the silence.

"What if it's worse than bad? What if it's...?" He let the words trail off.

Her breath seemed to lodge in her lungs. He was no longer discussing a fairy tale. The conversation had metamorphosed into something much more intimate. And dangerous. Suddenly feeling vulnerable, she rubbed her arms and chose her words carefully. "She'd listen to his explanation before passing judgment."

Nick remembered Sally's shock and dismay when she'd discovered his gruesome secret. "And then what?" Leaning against the edge of an adjacent desk, he folded his arms across his chest, the gesture almost defensive. "Would the beautiful princess still consider the warrior brave and noble if he told her, let's say, that he'd killed someone?"

His impassive expression had not changed, but the restrained torment edging his words squeezed at Stephanie's heart. "Isn't that what a warrior is trained to do?"

"Is he?"

"If it's expected of him, how can he be blamed?"

"What if the warrior has killed—" Nick wondered what drove him to continue this insanity "—a child?"

Stephanie ached with the desolation contained in that stark question. She knew the horror Nick alluded to was not an uncommon occurrence, that during combat civilians often got caught in the cross fire. She also knew that in some instances, children were trained to kill enemy soldiers. Much deadlier than regular troops, those seeming innocents could infiltrate enemy lines without raising suspicion. "I think he did what he had to do." Stephanie barely registered that she'd slipped into first person.

"Do you?" Nick smiled bleakly, reaching out and gently brushing a finger over her cheek before withdrawing his hand. "Anyone ever tell you you're very good at fantasies?"

"So I've been told." She searched his face, wincing at the hurt she sensed in him. "But this isn't one."

"No." His dark gaze ran down the length of her, taking in her protective stance. "Are you afraid of me?"

"Should I be?"

He rubbed the back of his neck, briefly squeezing his eyes shut. "Maybe you should."

Again the computer intruded with its demanding beep. She returned to it to insert the final disk, then rose from her chair and looked at Nick, taking in his haggard features. "Let's go sit over there," she suggested, gesturing toward a comfortable-looking couch sitting against the wall on the other side of the room. "You don't seem any too steady on your feet and I doubt I'd be able to keep you from doing serious bodily injury if you hit the floor."

The fact that he didn't demur, Nick thought, indicated just how much the past two days had gotten to him. He followed her, shrugging out of his jacket as he went. Tossing it aside, he rolled his shirtsleeves to his elbows and sprawled on the couch. He stretched his long legs out in front of him, leaned his head back and, exhaling heavily, closed his eyes.

Tucking one leg beneath her, Stephanie settled on the cushion beside him.

Nick could feel the warmth of her, smell the subtle scent he'd come to associate with Stephanie reaching out to him. Very dangerous to his limited self-control, he realized as he shifted to hide the physical evidence manifesting itself in the lower region of his anatomy.

"I think the incident with the child is a tragedy that happened a long time ago," Stephanie stated quietly. "Something else is troubling you tonight."

He waited a beat. "How do you know?"

"You're not a man to leave problems unresolved," she said simply.

Angling his head, Nick opened his eyes to pin her with an assessing stare. Her perception surprised him— and made him instinctively wary. "Sometimes you don't have a choice." He closed his eyes again, trying to shut her out. "I warned you before that it isn't smart to credit a man with noble qualities before he's proved he deserves them."

She disregarded his warning, unsure what possessed her to prod him into telling her things he obviously didn't want to divulge. "I'd guess it's much more recent—like something to do with why you were called in by the agency."

Along with being too damned tempting, Nick thought sardonically, Dr. Stephanie Harcourt could also be very persistent. The hellish events he'd tried to keep at bay slithered into his mind. His partner still hadn't checked in. No one had heard from him in almost a week. And none of Nick's contacts had been able to supply any information. Damn it, Slater should have listened, he thought in frustration, and gotten out of field work.

A couple of years ago, Nick had opted for undercover work in the "safer" arena of Washington's international politics, where more than a few of the dirtier deals were mapped out and finalized theoretically—with less physical danger. But Slater hadn't been able to let go. He'd continued to seek out the more-dangerous parts of each assignment.

"Maybe the warrior wants to protect the princess," Nick suggested. His voice sounded rusty even to his own ears.

"From what?"

He recalled in detail the scum he'd dealt with during the past two days, trying to find out what he could about Slater. "Modern-day dragons," he finally said.

"Shouldn't he tell her about them," she asked quietly, "so she'll know what to be wary of?"

Nick got up from the couch and walked over to the window. The sky had grown dark, he noticed absently. The only illumination inside the office was from a small area lamp near the desk where Stephanie had been working and from the faint blue glow of the monitor's screen. They lent an intimate atmosphere to the room.

Stephanie ached as she watched Nick silently grapple with whatever demon was pursuing him. When he didn't continue, she got up and followed him. This time she didn't allow herself to touch him.

The subtle fragrance and heat from her body wrapped around Nick. This wasn't the reason he'd come to her tonight, he told himself harshly. Or was it?

He pivoted to face her. "You keep pushing," he warned in a husky voice, "and you're going to learn more than you want to know."

"It helps to talk."

"You want to help?" He reached for her, surprised that his hands weren't quite steady. "Here's how you can help." His mouth was rough, not by intent but out of need—a burning, clawing need that demanded to be assuaged.

And she responded—without thinking, without question. It was as if, Stephanie thought dazedly, their kiss of several days ago had been a prelude to this moment.

He groaned, a harsh, grating sound, and forced himself to gentle the kiss, while at the same time deepening it. His hands came up to frame her face, angling her head so that he could delve deeper into her welcoming warmth.

Stephanie was unprepared for the onslaught of sensual need and unconsciously leaned into him, returning his passion.

Her response was as sweet as he remembered and far sexier than any other in Nick's memory. It served to push his already tenuous control another notch closer to the edge. He aligned his hips to hers in a futile attempt to warn her.

Stephanie made a soft mewling sound at the pressure of his arousal straining so intimately against her pelvis.

Her moan momentarily cut through Nick's clouded senses. Reluctantly he lifted his head. "Sorry. This isn't what I intended," he muttered, his voice hoarse. "Going without sleep for thirty-six hours plays hell with a man's self-control."

Stephanie slowly opened her eyes to search the glittering depths of his. There had been a hidden desperation in his apology. Instinctively, and without understanding exactly why, she tightened her arms around his neck and tried to pull his mouth back to hers.

Nick groaned at her silent acquiescence. Calling on what little sanity he still retained, he forced his hands to release their hold on her face. Once he let go of her, it wouldn't be so difficult to step away from her. Would it? The confusion he glimpsed in her before she concealed it disturbed him in ways he didn't want to define.

Her protective instinct came to Stephanie's aid. Her arms slid from around his neck—funny, she didn't remember putting them there—and she backed away. Clearing her throat, she pushed her glasses back into place. "I guess we'd better stick to talking."

He was surprised how bereft he felt, as if a vital part of him had been amputated. He couldn't shake the almost-overpowering urge to pull her to him, to erase the wounded look that darkened her eyes. Instead he raked his hands through his hair. "It seems finesse is another casualty of being a warrior."

The guttural remark told Stephanie that Nick had returned to their earlier conversation. "Are there many?"

"Too many." The grim sound he made barely passed for a laugh. "Like suddenly making stupid mistakes. And causing people around him to get hurt."

"I'm certain our warrior helps far more than he harms."

"Maybe. But even the best eventually burn out, lose their edge." He paused. "Become less vigilant."

Realizing her glasses were badly smudged, Stephanie removed them and set them aside. "Are you going to tell me what you're really talking about, or are we going to keep evading the issue?"

He wished to hell he could. "Let's just say that someone who depended on me is missing and may be in danger—possibly because I wasn't paying attention to what was going on." He knew Slater took unnecessary risks. Somehow Nick should have kept an eye on his partner.

Even as she moved toward him, Stephanie knew she was making an irrevocable decision.

And as soon as she was within touching distance, Nick reached for her, dragging her into his arms. "I warned you," he muttered raggedly.

Chapter Nine

"I've had about as much as I can handle tonight, Dr. Stephanie Harcourt." Nick said it quietly, but there was more than a warning in his words. "I'm going to kiss you again." His hand slid into her hair, positioning her head to receive his mouth, but he didn't lower his lips to hers. "If you object, this is your last chance to run like hell."

Stephanie studied the naked emotions carved on his face. "Would it do me any good?" she asked unsteadily.

He watched her intently for several heartbeats. "Not in this lifetime."

She couldn't retreat. The problem, she admitted silently before rational thought deserted her, was that she wanted this with every fiber of her being.

His earlier desperation had increased to an unmanageable degree. Nick knew it.

Stephanie sensed it as soon as his mouth settled roughly over hers. The kiss was hard and hungry. And she ceased thinking and simply responded.

Nick discarded any hope of stopping. He needed her. His right hand sought her breast. And she pushed against his palm, offering herself to him. She was firm and perfectly shaped—and the imprint of her burned into his senses.

Stephanie felt her nipples pucker in aching arousal as his fingers explored her urgently. She'd never encountered anything of this magnitude and her limited experience with men left her without a clue what was expected of her. She simply surrendered to her own clamoring senses—and his overriding need.

Nick sensed her uncertainty, even as her eager response played havoc with his dwindling self-control. A distant corner of his brain told him that he wanted Stephanie in a way that went far beyond the physical coupling of their bodies. He needed her—needed her with a desperation he couldn't remember ever experiencing before. And he was incapable of refusing what she so willingly offered. The realization terrified him. Yet the truth of it couldn't dampen the fire racing through him.

He lifted his mouth just a scant inch. "I want to see you." His hand fumbled with the row of tiny buttons running down the front of her dress. His clumsiness surprised him, since he couldn't remember a time when he hadn't been in complete control with a woman.

Brushing the material aside, he looked down at her almost-bare breasts, covered with the tiniest scrap of creamy lace. And groaned. *Sexy.* Again, not what he'd imagined she'd choose. There were hidden facets to this woman that would probably bring him to his knees should she ever decide to try. The muted light lent a translucent sheen to her skin, making her appear almost ethereal.

Maybe he was hallucinating, he thought in resignation.

"Maybe you're a fantasy," he said aloud.

"No," Stephanie assured him, distantly shocked at how uninhibited, how wanton she felt at this moment. "Very real, very human."

"Thank God." Nick let out a husky laugh, the sound dark with erotic promise. "I want flesh and blood." He leaned against the desk, cradling Stephanie between his widespread legs, and bent to take a lace-covered nipple into his mouth.

The shock of Nick's mouth on her breast coupled with the feel of his hard arousal pressing low against her abdomen stole her breath. Threading her fingers into his thick, dark hair, Stephanie anchored herself to him. Her breath grew shallow and her heart beat heavily against her ribs.

He groaned low in his throat and pulled back to release the front clasp of her bra. "Whatever you are," he muttered thickly, "God, I need..."

She wasn't certain Nick was aware he'd spoken aloud. His sexual hunger was consuming, but it was his underlying emotional need that overwhelmed Stephanie. She'd never been needed just for herself before—and Nick's need went deeper than merely physical. It was intoxicating. The knowledge wrapped around her heart, pulling her in. And it extinguished any remaining reservations.

The effect was soul shattering.

She reached for the buttons on his shirt, the fine cotton fabric now hopelessly wrinkled, whether from her questing hands or his long grueling day, she couldn't say. The feel of his heated flesh beneath her palms was surprisingly erotic, considering that she'd seen his bare chest countless times over the past several weeks.

"If you are a dream," he said hoarsely, "I hope I never wake up." He pushed the lace of the bra aside, freeing her breasts. His breath lodged in his throat. Her breasts were exquisite—even better than the vivid images that had tormented him each time he saw her in one of her prim swimsuits. Then he touched their soft fullness, lifting them, stroking the nipples with his thumbs, bringing them to taut peaks.

Stephanie bit her lower lip to contain the excitement melting the very center of her. Matching him step for step, she struggled awkwardly with the zipper of his slacks until his own eagerness drove Nick to take over the task. Unfastening his belt, he fumbled with the zipper and, with a grimace, freed himself. With his other hand he bunched up the material of her full skirt to give him access to the apex of her thighs.

His fingers slipped inside the fragile barrier of her panties. And he found her, hot and wet. The confirmation of her readiness proved the ultimate challenge to his control. His one consuming thought was to sink into her sweetness, to lose himself in her. To become a part of her. And Stephanie seemed to agree, helping him remove that one final obstacle between them.

Nick tried to master the desire that screamed for swift release. And her hunger matched his. He'd always prided himself on being a considerate lover, his expertise a measure of compensation. He might be incapable of giving a woman a child, but he sure as hell could give her good sex.

But tonight was different—tonight he wanted more than primitive pleasure. He wanted this experience with Stephanie to be special. Something she couldn't wash from her senses. More importantly, he wanted to strip the memory of any other man from her mind.

He didn't bother to question where this primal instinct came from.

Squeezing his eyes shut, he fought for some measure of control, then opened them and focused on her face. It was flushed, he noted, her mouth softly swollen from his kisses, her eyes dilated with the same passion that raced through his veins. But the uncertainty he read there did something to him. He lowered his head and slowly, deliberately, ran his tongue over her lower lip, then the upper, hovering just short of a complete kiss.

Stephanie moaned softly and closed her eyes, savoring the sensual mark that was uniquely Nick's, no longer fighting the emotions washing through her.

Nick withdrew his hand from her. With one impatient swipe, he cleared the clutter from the desk and gently laid Stephanie back against the smooth, cool surface. He unfastened the remainder of her buttons, then pushed aside her dress, fully exposing her body to his hungry gaze. He ran an unsteady hand reverently across each breast, then downward over her taut stomach. In the dim light, her smooth, supple skin showed no trace that she'd ever been pregnant. But she had.

He'd created a child with this woman—unwittingly, but it had happened all the same. The certainty of it stirred a feeling of awe in him, a possessiveness that shook him to the core.

Her body had given Jason life. And for a split second Nick was swamped by the fierce satisfaction that no other man had fathered her child. But the satisfaction was followed swiftly by an aching loss. He'd missed that, like he'd missed so many things in his son's life. He'd never see Stephanie swollen with his child. What had she looked like pregnant? he wondered. Had she shown her pregnancy right away or concealed it well? The unanswered questions served only to increase the heaviness in his groin.

Nick moved his hand lower, into the intimate patch of tawny curls. Stephanie shifted sinuously, welcoming his touch with a low moan. And his tenuous control snapped.

He positioned himself between her thighs, then froze. Her response, the scent of her, all his conflicting thoughts and emotions tonight had almost made him forget what he never allowed himself to forget. Almost. At the last possible moment he made himself reach into his pocket for the small foil packet.

Then in one smooth motion he slid into her. She met his thrust without hesitation. It didn't last long, the intensity—and his need—overriding his desire to prolong the encounter. He was able to hold off just long enough to feel the beginnings of her soft convulsions, that triggered his own explosive climax, and they rode the maelstrom out together.

For countless moments afterward, the only sound that registered on Stephanie was their labored breathing. Her body felt boneless—and foreign to her, as if it were no longer her own, as if what had just transpired between them had changed her irrevocably. She'd felt an inexplicable connection with this man ever since she'd met him, and tonight that connection had been extended to an even deeper, more-primitive level.

In slow increments, the fact that she was sprawled over her desk in anything but a dignified manner seeped into her consciousness. She couldn't recall how they'd ended up in this position. She was aware of Nick levering himself onto one elbow and felt burned by his gaze. She slowly opened her eyes, staring into his unreadable face.

Mortification washed over her in a cold wave. Being able to fault him for her uninhibited actions, she realized, would ease her embarrassment immeasurably. But she couldn't. Her innate sense of honesty reminded her that she'd wanted everything he'd demanded of her. And more. She closed her eyes.

Nick muttered a succinct oath and felt a peculiar ache deep in his chest. She looked so damned vulnerable. "Did I hurt you?" he finally asked, his voice low and rough.

Stephanie felt him studying her but refused to look at him, pulling what dignity she could muster around her like a protective shroud. "No." *At least not physically.* She gently shoved against his shoulders to free herself. After several heartbeats he reluctantly eased away.

She scrambled off the desk and quickly adjusted her clothes. Her papers, she noted absently, were now hopelessly scattered. A large number of them had fallen to the floor, and to fill the awkward silence, she began haphazardly sorting through the chaos. Out of the corner of her eye, she saw Nick straighten his own clothing, then spear his fingers through his hair.

A moment later his large hands stilled hers.

She closed her eyes and let the folder fall back to the floor.

"Stephanie," he prompted gently.

"Please. Let's...not talk about it." She felt too raw. Too fragile. The last thing she could handle right now was a discussion of what had just happened between them.

Part of him, Nick had to admit, was pathetically grateful for the reprieve. But he wanted to comfort her, to banish the reserve that had replaced her earlier spontaneity. Damn! He didn't know what to say or do to make amends, without running the risk of making things worse. So he simply let her go.

She immediately returned to the chore of collecting her scattered papers.

When the last folder had been retrieved, he took it from her hand and tossed it onto her desk, his gaze returning to her. "Now what?" he asked. The enormity of what they'd just done seemed to hang between them like an ominous shadow.

She glanced around the familiar room, knowing she'd never again view her office in quite the same light. "Can we get out of here?"

A muscle jumped in his jaw. "Let's go." He waited while she quickly closed down the computer and gathered her things.

As they started to leave, she hesitated, then looked at him. "Thank you."

"For what?" Nick asked gruffly, giving her a lopsided smile that didn't quite reach his eyes. "You like being attacked?"

Her laugh was shaky and slightly embarrassed. "No. For protecting me." She took a deep breath. "I'm afraid any evidence of responsibility on my part was sadly...lacking." She'd found it oddly touching that Nick had remembered.

Her words slammed into him, and he felt a stab of guilt. "No problem."

What else could he say? That he carried the damn things around with him as an example to some of the college kids he occasionally coached, an example that said if they wouldn't practice abstinence, at least be prepared? His mouth lifted in a self-mocking smile. Should he tell her that it had been so long since he'd needed one himself that they were lucky the thing hadn't broken? That he never, never had unprotected sex? He might be sterile, but he wasn't stupid.

But that wasn't why he'd remembered tonight, a little voice taunted. Tonight, he'd remembered for the sole purpose of perpetuating his deception. Because he hadn't wanted to explain that she needn't worry. That he couldn't get her pregnant.

Even if she'd wanted it.

He felt an ache in the region of his heart, and he ground his teeth. "Ready?"

She nodded, disturbed by his grim expression.

"Good," he said, steering her toward the door. "Let's get you home before I do any more damage." When they reached her car, she handed him the keys.

He accepted them without comment. He'd have no trouble driving. Despite his lack of sleep, he was now wide awake. It would probably be a hell of a long time before he had another decent night's rest.

The dashboard lights softly illuminated the interior of the Mercedes. Stephanie concentrated on the mechanical hands of the clock as if it were a lifeline. It read 12:23 a.m. Nick hadn't spoken since they'd left the lab compound, and she was hesitant to break the silence between them.

"You should do this for a living," Nick said finally.

Stephanie glanced at him sharply. "Pardon?"

"Weave fantasies about princesses and warriors."

"In a way," she told him after a brief pause, "I suppose I do." She bit her lip and shifted on the seat beside him, unintentionally drawing his gaze away from the road to rest on her.

The dim light didn't keep Nick from noticing how the fabric of her dress had stretched taut over her breasts. He swallowed hard, remembering the feel of them in his hands, then forced himself to focus on simply driving. "I hope you choose your audiences carefully," he said, his voice rough.

Stephanie absently played with the box of computer disks in her lap. "My fantasies aren't meant for adults."

"No?" He smiled crookedly. "If tonight's any example, maybe you should rethink that." Again his gaze left the road to roam over her. "They're potent."

"My typical audience is quite young," Stephanie told him, ignoring the innuendo. "And usually being read to by a parent."

Or an uncle, he added silently, recalling the contents of her home library. "You write children's books."

She nodded, not surprised that he'd guessed. It was just one more piece of personal information to add to all the others he seemed to collect at random. "You're the only person, other than my editor, who knows."

"Not even your family?" he asked.

"No."

Nick considered this for several moments. "How do you know I won't reveal your little secret?"

Good question, she thought. *One more test.* "I guess I don't, do I?"

A part of him very badly wanted to ask why she'd chosen to tell him. But he didn't. "Why haven't you told anyone?"

Stephanie watched the oncoming headlights on the Washington Beltway's inner loop slide by like a string of loosely strung diamonds. "Keeps anyone from trying to interfere."

"Interfere how?"

"By trying to change my mind," she said. "I write because I want to. Not because it's expected of me." She turned her head so that she could study his profile, willing him to understand. "This is one part of my life nobody controls but me."

He took a deep breath, then expelled it. "Control's important."

"Then you understand?"

"I understand." The glow from the dashboard lights set his features in harsh relief. "When a man loses control of a situation, people he's responsible for can get hurt."

He spoke almost as if he'd forgotten she was there. Stephanie waited for him to continue. When he didn't, she said softly, "This is what you were talking about earlier this evening."

He cast her a startled glance. "Yeah. I guess it is." The helplessness that had plagued him for the last few days returned. He rolled his shoulders to relieve the tension. "A problem with an assignment my partner and I've been working on."

"I thought the investigation at the lab was your current assignment."

Damn, he was in worse shape than he'd thought. It wasn't like him to make a slip like that. "But not the only one," he said, scrambling for an explanation that wouldn't raise more questions that it answered. "We'd reached the sit-around-and-wait stage on the other one. It was up to the other guys to make a move. And that wasn't expected for a while.'' He rolled his shoulders again. "So the agency assigned me to the lab investigation.'' He was getting dangerously good at lying, he reflected in disgust.

"But something's happened?"

"My partner. No one's heard from him for a while.'' And Nick couldn't shake the guilt that this was somehow his fault. If he hadn't been so wrapped up in finding his son, Slater wouldn't be in danger right now. A part of Nick knew the feeling was irrational, but it was there all the same. It was partly because of his confusion over this turn of events that he'd ended up on Stephanie's doorstep at nine o'clock at night. He felt as though he was no longer in control of his life.

"Maybe he just hasn't had time to contact you,'' Stephanie offered, sensing the inner tension in Nick and experiencing a profound desire to ease it in some manner.

"It's possible.'' There was a brief silence. "But highly unusual for him.''

"You think he's in danger.''

Nick noted that she'd made a statement, not asked a question. She was getting disturbingly good at reading him. "Maybe.''

"I'm sorry,'' she said quietly, but it sounded inadequate even to her own ears.

"He's been my partner since the agency recruited me.''

And Nick cared deeply for the man. Stephanie could hear it as clearly as if he'd said the words aloud. "What will you do?''

He laughed, but without humor. "There's not a damned thing we can do but wait.''

Nick's hand struck the steering wheel with such force that Stephanie jumped. She understood how frustrating waiting could be, the feeling of being powerless in the face of forces that controlled you. The nature of her own work often caused grinding delays at the worst possible times. Wasn't that why she'd been so upset about Nick's intrusion into her current project? But that seemed insignificant when compared to worrying about the safety of someone you cared for. The thought made her ache for Nick.

"I hope everything works out all right," she said to scatter the thickening silence.

"It will," he said flatly and without reservation.

Stephanie shivered. The determination in his tone was irrevocable. She recalled what Alex had said about Nick. Something to the effect that he would be good to have at your back, but she'd hate to have him for an enemy.

Stephanie had no doubt that Nick fought hard for those he cared about deeply. What would it be like to be numbered among those he cared for? she wondered, experiencing a painful little catch in her heart. On the other hand, she was certain beyond doubt, that being the one who came between him and the person he cared for would be extremely unwise.

On some level she could comprehend what he was going through. She knew what she'd do should someone try to come between her and Jason or Alex.

She had no trouble imagining what Nick would do.

Stephanie was immeasurably relieved when they finally reached her house. For once the imposing structure seemed like a welcoming refuge. Just a few minutes more, she told herself as she hurried up the steps to the front door, and she could escape to the privacy of her room—and perhaps regain some measure of calm.

But after stopping her car in the driveway, Nick didn't go to his own vehicle. Instead he'd followed her up to the front door, waiting patiently a half step behind her. Before she had an opportunity to get the key into the lock, Alex pulled the door open.

"Welcome home," her sister called cheerfully.

"You found my note?" Stephanie asked, feeling a small amount of guilt at arriving later than she'd indicated. Nick stepped out of the shadows, placing his hand at the small of her back. His touch was meant to be polite, she was certain, but it sent a sizzle along her already sensitized nerve endings with alarming speed.

"Right where you left it," Alex said, moving back so they could come inside. All the while she assessed Nick with her astute green eyes. "Mr. Saxon," she greeted.

"Ms. Harcourt."

With an inner sigh, Stephanie walked into the entrance hall. To a stranger, Alex might simply be displaying social interest. But Stephanie knew better. Anyone wandering into Alex's range was subjected to her unique brand of keen observation, a search for weaknesses and closely guarded secrets. She had a lot in common with Nick, Stephanie decided.

"Your note said you'd be home sooner," Alex commented, closing the door behind them. "I was a little concerned."

"Sorry. It took a little longer than I . . . expected." Stephanie headed for the great room, aware of Nick's gaze on her back as he followed at a slower pace.

"Isn't she a little old for a curfew?" Nick asked casually, evaluating Alex in much the same way as she had evaluated him.

"Tsk, tsk, Mr. Saxon," Alex said good-naturedly. "It isn't politically correct to refer to anyone over thirty as old."

"I'll try to keep that in mind." He smiled as he spoke, but his eyes remained cool.

"Is that you, Mom?" Jason called from the second-floor hallway.

"Yes, it's me. What are you still doing up at nearly one o'clock in the morning?" Stephanie asked, casting a mildly chastising look at Alex, who simply shrugged and tried unsuccessfully to look sheepish.

"Is Nick with you?"

"Right here, champ," Nick answered, watching his son bound down the stairs two at a time. Jason stopped in front of him, and Nick couldn't resist the urge to affectionately ruffle his hair.

"I wanted to see Nick," Jason said, glancing at his mother as if to say the explanation should be obvious. Then he turned to Nick. "When are you going to take us out on your boat?"

Jason's enthusiasm sent a pang through Stephanie. He enjoyed being with Nick so much. Even though she'd had to accept the fact that her son sometimes might need to be around a man, she couldn't avoid a brief twinge of envy.

Nick hunkered down so that he was at eye level with Jason. "We'll set something up just as soon as possible, okay?"

Jason looked crestfallen. "I guess that means it won't be for a while, huh?"

Stephanie felt Nick's unreadable gaze on her and remembered the way he'd looked as he talked about his missing partner, the concern she'd read in his face, heard in his voice. A new rush of conflicting emotions washed through her. "We'll talk about it tomorrow," she told her son.

"Couldn't we decide now?" he asked, looking hopefully at Nick.

"To bed, young man," she said firmly, patting him on the rump. "I'll be up in a minute to tuck you in."

"Okay." Jason acquiesced with reluctance. "'Night, Nick."

"Good night, Son. I'll see you soon, I promise." Nick wondered if anyone else noticed his unconscious slip of tongue. Stephanie might have missed it—she was still rattled from what had happened earlier—but Alex, casually standing off to one side, was studying the scene with more than a little interest. He struggled against the urge to hug Jason, tell him that he wasn't going to disappear from his life. Being this tired Nick told himself, as he watched his son disappear up the stairs, could prove hazardous.

Stephanie read Nick's weariness in the lines of fatigue on his hard face, and her heart went out to him. "You never did get anything to eat," she said softly. "Can we fix you something?"

"Thanks, but that isn't—"

"Go on up and take care of Jase, Sis," Alex interjected, stepping forward. "I'll take care of your guest."

Stephanie hesitated, then started toward the stairs. "Good idea. If I don't make sure Jason winds down, he'll be up the rest of the night."

"So you're hungry," Alex said to Nick, leading the way to the kitchen. "What would you like?"

"Anything." Nick's eyes narrowed slightly. "I think the last time my stomach saw food was around... I'm not certain when."

"How about BLTs?" she asked as she began assembling the necessary ingredients.

"Sounds good to me. Need help?"

Alex shook her head. "I've got it covered." She gestured toward a nearby stool. "Have a seat."

Nick sighed heavily and sat. "Okay, what's on your mind?"

She glanced up quickly from her task of layering bacon in a microwave pan. "You believe in being direct."

Most of the time, he thought sardonically. "I've found it saves time."

"Good." She slathered mayonnaise on two freshly toasted slices of bread. "I had you investigated."

For a full ten seconds, Nick didn't respond. "And?"

Alex laid down the knife and watched his face closely. "You're not surprised? Upset?"

"Would it do me any good?"

She studied him for a moment longer, then returned to her task. "No."

Nick shrugged and picked up a piece of crisp bacon, casually examining it before taking a bite. "Then why waste the effort?"

"Interested in what I learned?"

"I'm certain you'll tell me if you want me to know."

"Right." She glanced at his expressionless face. "I know you're a hell of a lot more than you appear."

He smiled slightly. "Isn't everyone?"

"Especially those with highest government clearance."

Nick whistled softly. "You have impressive sources."

"And you have impressive credentials." She placed the sandwich on a plate and set it in front of him.

"And your conclusions?" Nick asked before taking a bite.

Alex hesitated. "That you can be trusted. At least with state secrets. I'm still working on why you suddenly dropped into Stephanie's and Jason's lives."

"Hasn't Stephanie explained it to you?"

"I know the official explanation." She held up a pitcher. "Iced tea?"

He nodded. "But you doubt it."

"I have a hunch," Alex said, pouring two glasses and handing one to Nick. "And I always follow my instincts."

"I see. What do your instincts tell you?"

"That you're far more involved in Stephanie's life than necessary."

"And you're in a position to know that?" Nick asked, wondering where this conversation was leading.

Alex pinned him with clear green eyes, and Nick could swear he detected something like amusement in them. "Don't ever doubt it. I haven't been on the police force as long as I have without learning a little something about undercover investigations. And the one you're conducting at Stephanie's lab doesn't warrant this much attention."

"So you've concluded that I have some... ulterior motive?"

"I think you have an interest in my sister and Jason that goes beyond what's needed for this investigation, yes."

Nick took a long drink of tea and tried to check the knot of apprehension forming in his belly. "Is this conversation going somewhere?"

"Just want to make certain you know what you're dealing with here." She took a sip of her own tea. "Most of the people in Stephanie's life want a piece of her. There are damn few who see beyond her use as a commodity."

Which explained, Nick realized, why Stephanie always seemed to question his motives. Of course, a little voice taunted, in his case she had every right to. He pushed his plate aside. "Why are you telling me this?"

"There's no doubt you've been good for Jason. And my sister's been more—" Alex searched for the right word "—alive the last few weeks than I can ever remember." She lifted a shoulder. "I guess what I'm saying is that I approve of whatever it is you're doing for her. She deserves some happiness. God knows, she's been allowed little of it. She's spent most of her life fulfilling someone else's dream."

Nick had trouble drawing in a clear breath. He should warn her not to give her blessings too quickly, that they might backfire in her face. And Jason's. He couldn't bring himself to imagine how Stephanie would be affected should she ever learn—when she learned—what he was keeping from her.

Alex stood and began clearing the counter. "All I ask is that you don't hurt Stephanie."

"Do I hear my name being taken in vain?" Stephanie asked, walking into the kitchen. "Sorry it took so long." Sensing some tension hanging in the air, she glanced from Alex to Nick. "Did you get enough to eat?"

"Couldn't eat another bite," Nick assured her with absolute honesty.

"Well, how many stories did you tell him tonight?" Alex asked, amusement dancing in her eyes.

Stephanie laughed, a breathy little huff that Nick found sexy as well as captivating. "He wanted a new one," she said, pouring herself some iced tea. "That takes a little longer."

Yeah, Nick thought. He knew how that went. He could gladly listen forever to Stephanie's fantasies. They had touched him in ways he hadn't been touched in a long while.

She set down her glass and looked at Nick. "Would you mind terribly going up to tell Jason good-night? I hate to ask, but he's very insistent."

Nick's heart seemed to expand inside his chest, and it took him a moment to clear the lump of feeling from his throat. "No problem," he said, standing. "Just show me the way."

He felt as if he were riding an emotional roller coaster. He'd feared that after what had happened tonight, she might not want him around any longer.

"Thank you," Stephanie said, not hiding her relief. Was she making a grave error allowing Nick to move even further into Jason's life?

He was quiet as he followed her up the stairs. Finally he asked, "Did you expect me to refuse?"

They were just outside Jason's door before she answered. "I can honestly say I never know what to expect where you're concerned." She hung back and let him go in alone. Hugging her arms around her waist, she leaned against the doorjamb, unashamedly watching.

Jason's room was large and swathed in the soft glow of a night-light. Toys and gadgets, numerous enough to fulfill the wishes of most any little boy, were scattered like friendly sentinels throughout. His favorite "toy," a full-size computer much like the ones Stephanie worked on here and at the lab, sat silent in one corner. His bed was located close to a large window that overlooked the side grounds. Eyes closed, Jason was snuggled under a rumpled sheet and lightweight blanket.

When Nick settled his large frame on the edge of the bed, Jason turned his head on the pillow and smiled up at him. "Hi," he said in a sleepy voice. "I didn't know whether you'd come or not."

"Why wouldn't I?" Nick asked, straightening the bedding and smoothing it under the child's arms and across his chest.

Jason fiddled with a corner of the covers. "I thought maybe you might be too busy," he said softly.

Nick picked up one of Jason's small hands in his much-larger one and held it for several seconds. "Sometimes adults have to do things that are very important even when they'd like to be doing something else," he said quietly.

From her vantage point near the door, Stephanie could easily see Jason's face. But Nick's head was angled away from her, his expression concealed. There was something so heart-wrenchingly sweet about watching this strong man awkwardly trying to reassure her son.

"Yeah, I know. That's what Mom tells me sometimes."

"And kids have to try to understand."

Jason nodded and sighed, the sound holding reluctant acceptance. "It's just that I really like doing things with you."

Stephanie's heart twisted, and she felt unexpected tears gather at the back of her eyelids. Jason had always been mature beyond his years, in part because of his high IQ. By trying to spare him some of the heartache she'd experienced growing up, had she created an entirely different set of problems for him? Was that why he felt driven to beg a man he'd known only a few short weeks to spend time with him?

"And I like to do things with you," Nick told him, his voice sounding oddly raspy.

Frowning slightly, Jason considered that for a minute. "Will it be a long time before we can do something together again?"

Nick seemed to be choosing his words carefully. "Sometimes when we want something very badly, that's when we have to be the most patient of all." He squeezed Jason's shoulder, then ruffled his hair. "I'll work it out just as soon as I can. But don't hassle your mom about it, okay?"

Jason smiled again. "'Kay."

"Before you know it we'll be out there sailing on the Bay. I promise."

"'Night, Nick," he said, rolling over on to his side and closing his eyes.

"Good-night, Son." He gently drew the covers up around Jason's shoulders, then stood beside the bed, looking down at the boy.

When Nick turned in her direction, the emotion carved on his face was almost too painful for Stephanie to look at. She moved a couple of feet down the hall, struggling to control her reaction.

He stepped into the hallway, and she pulled the door closed, indicating that he should follow her downstairs.

When they reached the first-floor landing, she turned and looked up at him. From what he'd told her tonight, she'd guess that he'd been without sleep for going on forty-eight hours, and yet he'd answered a young boy's persistent questions with exquisite patience. "Thank you," she whispered.

"My pleasure," Nick said, studying her. "I won't be around for a while."

She nodded, searching his dark, unreadable eyes.

"I'll stop by the lab when I get a chance." He looked at her for long seconds, then lifted his hand and skimmed the pad of a finger over her full lower lip. "Will you come sailing with us as soon as I can work it out?"

"Yes." His face was etched with fatigue and something else Stephanie couldn't quite identify. For some curious reason she was reluctant to see him leave. There was so much unresolved between them. True, that was primarily her fault. She'd been the one who hadn't wanted to discuss what had happened between them tonight. As the erotic images swamped her, Stephanie felt her cheeks warm.

Nick's eyes dilated almost as if he'd read her mind. "I better go," he said gruffly.

"Would you like to sleep here tonight?" The words were out before she'd thought about them.

One side of Nick's mouth turned up in a provocative smile. "Is that an invitation?"

Stephanie felt her blush deepen, but she held his gaze. "Yes," she said softly. "To sleep. In a guest room. Alone."

His gaze, heated now by the shared sensual memories, roamed over her face, eventually coming to rest on her mouth. "Now that doesn't sound like much fun."

Instinctively she swayed toward him. "Are you sure you wouldn't like to stay?" she asked, realizing that he was declining her invitation. He smiled, a genuine smile that crinkled the corners of his eyes and made her heart turn over and slide to somewhere in the vicinity of her knees.

Don't look at me like that, he wanted to tell her. *Don't trust me too much.* "Don't tempt me," he said aloud, his voice rough. "You might regret it."

He'd like nothing better than to take her up on her offer, Nick thought longingly. But that would be too dangerous to his already raw emotions. It was too much like a happy family. Something he wasn't entitled to—not with this woman. Not with any woman who wanted children of her own.

Instinctively he knew that Stephanie would demand much more than a steady supply of hot sex from him. Tell her the truth, a rational part of him ordered. But something far stronger than mere self-preservation made him hold back.

That didn't stop him from placing his hands on her shoulders and pulling her against him. Slowly he lowered his head to hers and, with infinite care, positioned his mouth over hers.

The kiss was softly, shatteringly sweet and seemed to Stephanie almost a goodbye.

Too quickly, he lifted his head and stared down at her for several heartbeats. "I'll be in touch."

Chapter Ten

Stephanie watched Nick drive away before closing the massive front door. She leaned against it and inhaled deeply, trying to sort through all the conflicting emotions besieging her.

"Has he gone?"

Her sister's voice, unexpectedly dropping into the shadowy silence, startled Stephanie. "Yes." She pushed away from the door and began walking toward the stairs. "I think I'll go up to bed now."

"You okay?" Alex asked quietly.

Okay? Stephanie silently questioned. Did feeling more vulnerable than she'd ever felt in her life count as okay? So much had happened to her in such a short period of time. Mere hours. An eternity. "I'm fine," she lied. "Just tired. 'Night."

"'Night, Sis. Let me know if you want to talk."

"Thanks," Stephanie said, climbing the steps. As she passed her son's room, she peeked in to find Jason sleeping peacefully.

At least he was content, she thought, thanks to Nick. He'd reassured Jason with a few well-chosen words that would keep him in a happy state of anticipation for several days.

Once inside her own suite, Stephanie didn't stop until she'd reached her balcony and the balmy night air. She walked over to the small, powerful telescope and ran her hand over its protective housing. A smile played at the corners of her mouth. From this private retreat, she'd spent many hours teaching Jason the wonders of the night skies. Gazing at the stars had been a ready escape—even when she was a child. But apparently Jason needed more.

And Nick seemed to understand. With bittersweet clarity, Stephanie recalled the raw expression she'd witnessed on his face as he turned away from Jason's bed. Even now the memory had the power to bring tears to her eyes. Had Nick come to feel more for her son than simple friendship?

Stephanie paced the length of the balcony, missing the tranquillity she usually found here. More erotic memories bubbled to the surface of her mind, and she placed a hand over her stomach to calm the ripples of excitement they aroused.

Nick had reached out to her tonight for comfort, for forgiveness for a long-ago crime that wasn't his fault. She'd found it the most natural thing in the world to respond to his need. But there was something more. She sensed it.

Beneath his strength she was certain he carried some heavy burden, a burden that caused him deep pain. And whatever it was had to be even more hurtful for a man as compassionate as Nick. Which was probably why it had been inevitable that she fall in love with him.

The thought stopped her from breathing for a good ten seconds, and Stephanie felt panic rise to fill the void. Oh my God, she thought, that can't be. Could it? Of course it was. Why else would she have thrown caution to the wind and opened herself to this man? How else could he have stirred such uninhibited responses in her? Such unquestioning trust?

And she *had* come to trust him. First with Jason, then with her body, now with her heart. Had she made a grievous mistake? No! she told herself, fighting to contain the panic. Someone who'd suffered what Nick had, who was so loyal to his partner, who'd been so understanding with one small boy, who'd been such a considerate...lover—someone like Nick couldn't be capable of using another for his own purposes.

No, Stephanie reassured herself, she couldn't have misplaced her trust this time. Not when the man—Nick Saxon—had the power to devastate her as no other person ever could.

How could he have been so stupid? Nick wondered as he pointed his late-model Jeep south on Interstate 495. His reason for dropping by to see Stephanie in the first place had been to repair the damage he was afraid he'd done a few days ago with one simple kiss. Simple, hell. If it'd been all that simple, he wouldn't have been primed and ready to explode the first time he'd touched her tonight. How in hell was he going to repair *this*?

She probably thought he was a real basket case. Some crisis manager he'd turned out to be. For a man who was known for handling delicate situations, lousy didn't begin to describe his recent performance. But then again, he hadn't been prepared for Stephanie—for her understanding, her sympathy, her passion.

He prided himself on his self-control. By rigid self-discipline he'd hung onto his sanity and managed to come back from Nam minus most of the psychological horrors experienced by so many returning servicemen. But once home, he'd found it difficult to let go. That control had become too deeply ingrained, too much a part of him. So he'd nurtured it, turned it to his advantage in his work with the agency.

But the woman beneath the cool, regal exterior Stephanie so carefully presented to the world, the woman he'd been allowed only glimpses of before tonight, the woman who could weave fantasies that touched a man's soul, *that* woman challenged his control as no other.

And in his loss of control he'd learned things he hadn't wanted to know. Like the fact that this woman didn't lightly jump into bed with a man. He rubbed a hand over his face, recalling Stephanie's sweet abandon. Even in the heat of passion, in his rush to completion, he'd been conscious of her untutored responses.

Tonight he'd discovered he was dealing with someone who was vulnerable. Someone he could hurt badly. Someone he realized he very badly didn't want to hurt.

He was in deep trouble, he thought with irony. While he'd been busy charming his way into her life, Stephanie had quietly slipped past every one of his protective barriers and was now firmly entrenched in his own.

He'd deliberately not sought a permanent relationship since Sally. He knew firsthand how desperate a woman who wanted a child could become. His sterility had ultimately caused his wife's death. If she hadn't been so obsessed with getting pregnant, she wouldn't have gone out in a freak ice storm and been killed on her way to the fertility clinic.

And Stephanie had wanted a child of her own, Nick reminded himself, enough to resort to artificial insemination. She loved Jason. She probably wanted more children.

And that was something he couldn't give her.

He'd wanted—no, *needed*—Stephanie tonight. But he'd had no right to take advantage of the comfort she'd offered, no matter how great his need.

Yeah, he knew about control and controlling one's own destiny. He also knew about manipulation and deceit. And he knew what he'd do to any SOB who did to him what he was doing to Stephanie.

But he couldn't risk telling her the truth. Not yet. Nothing was settled between them. In fact, Alex's little talk earlier had brought home how much his deception could injure Stephanie. Funny, he'd never before thought of himself as a coward.

Guilt nagged at him. Well, there was one thing he could do to spare her. He wouldn't make love to Stephanie again, he silently swore, until he'd told her everything.

"And Slater's all right?" Nick braced one hand against the window frame in Matt's office and stared out at the Washington night lights glittering off the dark waters of the Potomac. He wondered grimly if he was ever going to do anything in daylight again.

"I haven't personally talked to him yet, but that's my understanding. He's heading back here for debriefing," Matt said. "I guess we'll know for certain then."

Nick nodded, feeling as if a great weight had been lifted off him. "Where does this leave us?"

"Not in the best position, that's damned certain." Matt released a heavy breath. "Word is our friends detained Slater as a warning that they won't appreciate any interference in their little scheme."

Nick delivered a pithy expletive and jammed his hands into his pockets. "We sure as hell can't sit back and let them dictate how this deal goes down." He swung around and eyed Matt sharply, noting that his friend looked like he'd aged ten years in the last few days. Nick knew how he felt.

"And we can't make any wrong moves, either. Our purpose here is to get to the brains behind this and put 'em out of business. We can't jeopardize the mission."

"To hell with the mission," Nick said succinctly. He withdrew his hands from his pockets and shoved all ten fingers through his hair. This was his fault. He should have seen it coming. He knew how reckless Slater could be. And Nick was allowing his personal life to interfere with his job—something he'd never done before. "Slater could still be in danger."

"Slater acted without orders. He knows the risks," Matt reminded him.

"We're talking about scum here, Matt. Illegal arms dealers. They sure as hell aren't going to play by the rules."

Matt nodded and rested his head against the back of his heavy, leather desk chair. It groaned under his six-foot-three-inch frame. "They want to make sure this supply of arms isn't sold to any other bidder before they've raised the money to buy it. Slater was their insurance. If we leave them alone, they'll leave us alone."

Nick dropped down into a chair across the desk from his superior. "So what's our next move?"

"They want to meet," he said. "Somewhere neutral."

"Just tell me when and where." He wanted this thing over. He never walked away from an operation before it was finished. *Just one more,* he told himself.

Matt eyed him critically. "I'm not sure you're up to it."

"What are you talking about?" Nick straightened in his chair, his eyes glittering dangerously. "My partner's involved here. Hell, all of us are. If they could get to us once, they can do it again." The feeling of helplessness that had plagued him since things started to go sour escalated to being close to panic. Damn, he hated it.

"I'm just suggesting that maybe it's too... personal. And with everything else on your mind, this might not be the best time."

"You bet it's personal." Nick pushed out of his chair and paced to the window again. "I know what arms like these can do to inexperienced ground troops—not to mention an unsuspecting civilian population."

Matt sensed the reckless determination in his friend and knew he wouldn't be dissuaded. "You can't right all the wrongs in this world," he told him quietly, "no matter how atrocious they might be."

"No. But if there's any way in hell I can keep this particular gang of arms dealers from causing the deaths of any more innocent bystanders, I'll do it." Like the kid who'd brandished a gun in the middle of a jungle a lifetime ago. A weapon he shouldn't have had. If he hadn't, maybe he'd still be alive. Once more the hellish image flashed through Nick's mind. Not only had a child died, but the act had shattered Nick so badly that he'd made a deadly mistake, allowing the enemy to sneak up on him.

And that mistake had cost him much more than a few months of his freedom. Nick shifted restlessly to cut off the flood of raw memories. As soon as this mission was completed, he wanted out of the agency altogether. No more dangerous assignments. He had a son who wanted to spend time with him. And Nick wanted nothing more in life than to spend time with his son.

Except maybe, no matter how hopeless it might be, to spend time with his son's mother.

He turned to face Matt. "Set it up."

"All right," Matt said slowly, watching Nick with a troubled gaze. "I'll let you know when and where."

It had been three long days since Stephanie had last had any contact with Nick. And even longer nights, she admitted candidly. But she'd expected it. She'd known that what he had to deal with would take time.

What she hadn't expected was the fact that she'd actually miss him around the lab. She'd gotten used to Nick turning up unexpectedly, his subtle and unexpected challenges, his sensual innuendos.

And Jason missed him, too. She glanced over at her son, working diligently at one of the computers. He'd been so antsy that she'd brought him to the lab, hoping to take his mind off Nick.

As if her thoughts had conjured him up, Nick suddenly walked unannounced into the room.

"Nick!" Jason exclaimed, scrambling from his chair.

Stephanie remained where she was, just watching Nick. Oh yes, she'd definitely missed him—far more than was smart. He still looked tired, she thought, his eyes shadowed with fatigue.

Jason made a beeline for him, and she watched Nick crouch down to catch the boy in a bear hug. A tight lump formed in her throat. After a moment Nick looked directly at her, but the glance he passed over her was cool, almost indifferent, before he returned his attention to Jason.

"Hi ya, sport," he said, his voice gruff.

As soon as he had learned Slater was safe, he'd wanted to come straight to Stephanie and share the news with her. The urge had been almost irresistible. And damned unsettling.

"Go back to what you were doing, Son," he told Jason. "I need to talk to your mom for a few minutes."

"Then can we talk about going sailing?" the boy asked hopefully.

"Jason," Stephanie said, a warning note in her voice.

He sighed theatrically. "Okay, Mom."

Nick squeezed Jason's shoulder. "We'll talk in a little while."

Jason nodded and headed back to the computer.

Nick walked over to Stephanie, stopping at the desk adjacent to hers. She watched a muscle ripple along the strong line of his jaw. His expression remained cool, certainly not that of a man remembering the fact that just days ago he'd made beautiful, heated love to her on the very desk he was standing beside. Her hand automatically went to her stomach to still the sensual flutter there. The passionate lover was gone; in his place was the remote professional. Maybe it was because Jason was in the room, she thought, trying to console herself.

"Is everything all right?" she finally asked, to break the silence.

"For the moment. I came by to tell you Slater's okay."

His thoughtfulness touched her. "Thank God."

"Yeah."

"But it's not finished yet," she stated.

He shook his head. "No."

"What's next?"

"We sit tight and wait." Nick was staggered by just how desperately he wanted to drag Stephanie out of her chair and kiss her senseless. He leaned against the desk, the same desk where mere days ago he'd lost himself in her body and her passionate response to their lovemaking.

Stephanie found she had to look away from Nick's intent eyes. Her gaze traveled around the lab, trying to find something else to fill the conversational void.

"I checked in with Security before I came by here," he finally said.

"Any new developments on this investigation?"

"Nothing," he said, still studying her. "No new episodes, no new evidence."

"Have you got any idea yet who's behind it?" She picked up a small piece of paper and began folding it into a geometric design, unconsciously running the tip of her tongue over her lower lip.

He should get out of there, Nick decided, before he did something stupid. "No," he said abruptly, and suddenly jerked away from the desk.

Stephanie felt a sharp pain in the region of her heart as she watched him stride across the room. He stopped behind Jason's chair, sliding his hands into his back pockets, then concentrating on what the boy was doing. After a few minutes, he asked Jason a question about what he was working on, gesturing to the screen.

Jason mumbled a reply, barely glancing up. They spoke in such hushed tones that she couldn't quite make out what was said. Finally Nick leaned down and said something that made her son stop what he was doing and laugh out loud.

Nick straightened and looked over at her. "You think you can get away from all this tomorrow to go sailing?" he asked.

Jason swiveled his chair around. "Oh, wow! Can we, Mom?"

The two of them had become so close, Stephanie reflected, again struck by how right they seemed together. "I think we can work it out," she said, trying to still a tiny flutter of unease.

Chapter Eleven

Nick's sailboat couldn't be considered ostentatious, Stephanie decided, even by conservative standards. It had a small, though well-equipped galley and in a pinch could sleep four people. Its hull was painted a brilliant white, with accents of deep blue. Rigged with two sails, the craft could easily be handled by one man. Which explained how Nick had gotten his calluses.

He obviously loved the sense of freedom sailing gave him. The sheer joy he took in having the wind whip his hair and sting his face was clear to anyone who watched him. And Stephanie took pleasure in watching.

After spending the better part of the morning teaching Jason the rudiments of sailing, Nick had dropped anchor off one of the small, secluded coves on the eastern shore of Chesapeake Bay. And Stephanie had gone below to get out of the sun and make lunch.

She put the finishing touches on several ham-and-cheese sandwiches, placed them on a platter and left it on the tiny counter. Then she headed up the short flight of stairs to the deck. As she reached the top step, she was momentarily blinded by the bright, late-August sun reflecting off the sparkling water. Stopping to allow her eyes to adjust, she heard the low murmur of voices. Nick was explaining the techniques of fishing to Jason.

Peeking over the enclosure that housed the narrow stairwell, she could observe the two of them, where they wouldn't notice her. Jason sat cross-legged, watching intently as Nick showed him how to bait a hook. Still in their swim trunks and abbreviated life jackets, both were tanned the same deep shade. They looked so relaxed sitting side by side. Jason might be a novice but he was obviously determined to learn from his new-found hero.

Stephanie again felt a pang of regret and something like guilt that it had taken Nick to show her just how much Jason needed to learn from a man. It had never occurred to her that Jason might be interested in fishing. It had taken Nick to point that out.

She shouldn't eavesdrop, she warned herself firmly. One of these days she was going to overhear something she might not want to know. But the cautionary voice couldn't force her to retreat from earshot or to make her presence known.

"You don't have any kids, do you?" Jason asked Nick.

Nick's hand stilled in the act of setting the bait. "I've got lots of nieces and nephews. Why do you think I don't have kids?" he asked casually, resuming his task.

"'Cause if you did, you probably wouldn't have time for me," Jason said matter-of-factly.

"Why wouldn't I have time for you?"

"'Cause my friends' dads don't have time for anybody but their own kids." Frowning in concentration, Jason took a piece of bait from the small bucket and tried to duplicate what Nick had done. "Did I do it right?" he asked, holding up his hook for Nick's inspection.

Stephanie felt tears sting her eyes as she watched Jason eagerly try to please Nick. And he was always patient with her child, never seeming to become aggravated by Jason's sometimes ceaseless questions. Even though she was aware he worked with other children, she couldn't quite comprehend the warm relationship that had developed between the two so quickly.

Nick examined Jason's hook. "Good job, Son." He picked up a nearby rag to wipe his hands, then reached over and squeezed his shoulder.

Jason looked up at him, his serious face questioning.

"No matter how many kids I might have," Nick told him quietly, "I promise I'll always have time for you."

Jason brightened immediately. "Yeah?"

"Yeah." He cast his line into the water, and Jason watched closely. "What do you know about your dad?" He asked after a minute.

A breath lodged painfully in Stephanie's chest. She should put a stop to this now, before it went any further. Nick had no right to ask Jason that. But something kept her rooted to the spot. He'd asked the question so easily, as if it were a perfectly natural subject for them to discuss.

"I don't have one," Jason said as he followed Nick's example and awkwardly attempted to throw his line into the water. It got tangled and only partially made it over the railing.

Setting his fishing rod aside, Nick went over to Jason to help. "You don't?" he asked casually, a muscle bunching in his jaw.

"Well, really I do." Jason giggled. "Everyone has a father." The impish twinkle left his eye. "But I can't know who mine is."

He sounded so grown-up, thought Stephanie, her heart aching. His last words had contained such a wistful note. And it caused the ache to expand into a knot deep within her.

"Why not?" Nick asked softly. He was out of his depth, Nick suddenly realized. He thought he knew how to handle kids. Hell, he'd been dealing with various ages of children for years, his family's or those he coached. But dealing with someone else's child—even a niece or nephew—was a far cry from dealing with your own son.

"Because Mom got me from a clinic."

Nick looked over at the boy and smiled. "She did, huh?" He'd wondered what Stephanie had told Jason about the circumstances of his birth. Now that he was about to find out, he wasn't certain he wanted to know. "What kind of clinic?"

Jason held tightly to his fishing pole, studying the cork float bobbing in the water. "Mom says it's where people go to get babies when they want one a whole lot but they don't have a dad."

Nick didn't speak for several long heartbeats. "Then your mom must love you an awful lot," he said in a low voice.

Jason thought about that, then smiled. "Yeah, I guess she does. Mom's okay. And I love her a lot," he added, as if he was somehow being disloyal. "But I sure would like a dad. Someday I'm going to find out about mine."

"You are, huh?" Nick said, his voice rough. "How're you going to do that?"

Jason tugged at his line to see if there might be a fish on it. "I'm not sure yet." He shrugged, as if he'd said more than he should. "But there's gotta be some way." He looked at Nick. "Don't you think?"

Stephanie exhaled the breath she hadn't been aware she was holding. She decided it was time to intervene, before things got completely out of hand. She blinked back the moisture gathering in her eyes and stepped into view.

"Lunch is ready, you two," she said with forced lightness. "Jason, why don't you go down and get washed up? You can have a sandwich when you're finished. Nick and I'll be down in a few minutes."

"But Mom," Jason said in a mildly disgruntled tone, "we were going to have fish for lunch."

"Oh yeah?" Stephanie peered into the bucket filled with bay water to hold their nonexistent catch. "And how many have you caught so far?"

Jason looked sheepish. "Well...not any, yet. But I bet we will in a little while. Won't we, Nick?"

"Probably not today. Go on, sport. Your mom has made lunch. Maybe next time we'll have better luck."

"Wow! Can we do this again?"

"You bet," Nick told him.

"Awright!" Jason set down the pole and tramped off toward the steps, looking back once before disappearing below deck.

Nick again wiped his hands on the rag. He didn't look at Stephanie. In fact, he didn't acknowledge her presence in any manner.

She had to tell him, Stephanie thought in resignation. She might not want to, but she couldn't simply leave it where Jason had left off, with all the unanswered questions that had to be buzzing around in Nick's head. She took a deep breath. Were there words that could explain why she'd chosen such an unorthodox method of conceiving? Would telling Nick about this be in Jason's best interest?

Once Nick had heard her explanation would he be put off by it? Put off by her?

"I guess you must be wondering what Jason was talking about," she said, running clammy hands down the sides of the shorts she'd pulled on over her swimsuit.

"It's none of my business," he said in a clipped tone.

Stephanie gave a shaky laugh. "I wouldn't want you to get the wrong idea." When he didn't comment, she wrapped her arms protectively across her middle, fiddling with the edges of her life jacket. "Jason was conceived by artificial insemination," she said in as even a voice as she could manage, considering the number of butterflies flying bomber runs in her stomach.

Fury bubbled up from deep within Nick. Fury at her, at himself, at fate. The same fury he'd carried since he'd learned what had happened eight years ago. But it was mixed with a longing so strong he didn't think he was capable of containing it. He clenched his teeth and began methodically collecting fishing gear.

"Would you like to know about it?" she asked.

Nick halted what he was doing and looked up at her, straight into her eyes and on into her soul. "I know." He closed the tackle box with a decisive snap.

She'd expected some sort of reaction from him. Now that she'd been confronted with it, she just wasn't certain how to handle it. She cleared her throat, contemplating how to proceed.

Nick rose to his full six-foot-plus height and began reeling in one of the lines. "What I don't know is why."

"Why?" Stephanie repeated. He sounded so angry, and for the life of her, she couldn't figure out why. Unless of course, he disapproved of the procedure on principle, and there were those who thought it wrong no matter what the reason or what the justification. But oddly enough she hadn't expected Nick Saxon to be one of them.

"Yeah, why?" He finished reeling in the second line, then put both rods away. "Was there suddenly a shortage of available men?"

Anger replaced her earlier confusion. "In my life? Yes! What's your point here, Nick?"

"Don't forget, I know you," he said, his voice dropping an octave. The gaze he swept over her burned like hot ice. "Intimately."

She took a step backward, as if he'd struck her.

Jamming his hands onto his hips, he inhaled sharply. "Sorry, that was out of line." He turned to face her, his eyes glittering in the afternoon sun. "Damn it, no it wasn't. You're a sexy, passionate woman. It's hard for me to believe you couldn't find a man willing to father your child."

She held her ground, refusing to allow the backhanded compliment to hurt. "You think that would've been preferable? Just go out and grab some guy and say, 'Pardon me, but if you could spare a few minutes, I'd like to get pregnant'?"

The image of Stephanie lying so openly, so seductively, under him several nights ago erupted into his mind's eye with the impact of an explosion. He didn't doubt she'd have all the takers she could handle. But the thought of her with any other man made him even angrier. "It would have at least given your son a father," Nick said, his voice now ominously low.

Like a knife to the heart, he'd found her Achilles' heel. "What business is it of yours?" she snapped.

For a full thirty seconds, Nick didn't speak. Not a muscle in his face moved. "Right again," he said, his voice without inflection. "I overstepped my bounds."

Damn right, Stephanie wanted to fling at him. *Jason doesn't need a father.* But she couldn't. Because he did. She knew now how much. Hadn't she heard Jason express that need just minutes ago? The fight went out of her. She moved to the bow of the boat out of Jason's earshot. Nick followed.

"No. You're right." She sat down on the narrow polished deck and drew her knees against her chest, encircling them with her arms. "It probably would've been better for Jason to know his father. But there was no one special in my life at the time." Or ever, she added silently.

"So what kept you from going out and finding someone?" Nick pinned her with eyes that demanded straight answers. "Or waiting until the right man came along?"

Stephanie grimaced. "Because I didn't have the luxury of time." Plus she'd never met a man who'd felt comfortable enough becoming involved with someone like her. *Until Nick Saxon.* The fleeting thought came from out of nowhere, and she quickly pushed it aside. That kind of thinking could open her up to all kinds of foolish hopes. Which she couldn't afford.

"What does time have to do with it? You were what, around thirty?" he asked, making it sound very much like an accusation.

She nodded, then sighed. "Regardless of what you may think, Nick, my decision to have a child was not spur-of-the-moment."

"Then explain it to me," he said, gritting his teeth against the vulnerable expression on Stephanie's face. He had a right to know, damn it. He had a right, he told himself grimly, to understand how she had come to have his child.

"The doctors told me if I didn't have a child then," she said, her voice without inflection, "most likely I never would."

That hit Nick like a fist to his midsection. Oh God, he knew how devastating that piece of news must have been. Closing the distance between them, he dropped down on the deck, facing her. "Do you want to talk about it?"

Why not? Stephanie thought. She'd come this far. She shifted, the movement conveying her discomfiture. "Have you heard of endometriosis?"

"I've heard the term, but can't say I know precisely what it means." He propped his arms over his raised knees, loosely clasping his hands in front of him, and waited for her to continue.

Stephanie looked away from his intent gaze and out at the water dancing against the lush shoreline a couple of hundred feet away. It gave her something to focus on while she talked. "Well, without getting too clinical, it's a disease that affects the female reproductive organs." She paused, mildly embarrassed at discussing something so personal with him. Right, she silently chided. Just days ago, Nick had been more intimate with her than any man had ever been. If not for his thoughtfulness that night, she might very well have gotten pregnant again. At the thought, a warm sensation curled through her.

"Go on," he said softly, while feeling like the lowest form of criminal. He had no right to violate her trust, urging her to reveal more and more of herself to him, listening to her deepest secrets. But he told himself he had no choice. He had to know how all this had affected her before he could confess his role in Jason's life.

"It started in my early twenties and each year seemed to get worse." Stephanie vividly recalled her struggle from month to month as she tried to ride out the unrelenting pain and the increasingly heavier bleeding, the bouts with anemia.

"Wasn't there anything that could be done—some medicine, some treatment?"

"I went to a battalion of specialists, the very best money could buy." Stephanie laughed without humor. "They tried every current medical procedure to correct, or at least modify, the condition. But nothing worked."

She glanced at Nick to gauge his reaction. He was concentrating on her as if what she had to say held something of vital importance. "I'm sorry," he said.

His voice had gentled, she noticed. She didn't want his pity. She simply wanted him to understand.

Nick wanted to pull her close and absorb her pain. Part of him wanted to tell her to stop, but another part had to know all of it. "You've come this far. Finish it."

"When they told me that I might not be able to have children . . ." Her voice trailed away.

"That's when you decided to have a child," he finished for her. *Our* child. The thought surprised him. He'd never thought of Jason as *theirs* before.

She nodded. "I'd always wanted children. Several, in fact." She smiled weakly and glanced at him, then away. Her smile turned bittersweet. "The thought of never having a child of my own was unthinkable." She'd wanted to fill her life with love and laughter—to make up for the years of loneliness.

A child of my own. The words kept beating inside his head. *She'd wanted a child of her own, her own, her own.* Not someone else's, he realized bleakly. He'd thought that might be the case. Confirming it hurt more than he'd anticipated.

"I agonized for months, but once I'd made the decision, I never regretted it." Stephanie looked directly into Nick's expressionless face. "Jason is the best thing that ever happened to me. If I'd done it differently, I wouldn't have him."

Yeah, Nick reflected, he couldn't argue with that. And without Stephanie, *he* wouldn't have a son. He felt a deep sense of loss that he hadn't been there when she'd made this life-altering decision. He hated thinking of her alone, with only her sister for support. He hated having missed so much of his son's life.

"Have you ever thought of having another child?" He had to find out, he told himself. He had to know.

"I'd love to," she answered without prevarication. "But this time I'd want the father around. I've come to realize that a child pays too dearly not knowing his father. Recently I've started to wonder if maybe I did Jason a terrible disservice." Her gaze sought his.

Nick felt a fragile hope wither. The irony of her words wasn't lost on him. A few short weeks ago he would have agreed wholeheartedly. But that was before he'd gotten to know his son. Before he'd gotten to know the mother of his child. Now he found himself wanting to reassure her, to banish the sad look that shadowed her soft gold green eyes.

Jason chose that moment to poke his head around the stairwell enclosure. "Can I play with Game Boy?"

"Good idea," Stephanie said, realizing that any other time she would have discouraged his playing the computer game. She was worried that he spent too much time with computers as it was. But this time she was grateful for the distraction. It would keep him occupied until she and Nick could finish their conversation. "You need to stay out of the sun. You've had enough for today."

"What about you two?" her son asked.

"We'll be down in a few minutes."

Jason looked first at Nick, then his mom, as if sensing something between them. "That means I should stay out of the way, right?"

Stephanie couldn't help but smile. Leave it to him to cut through all the small talk. "Something like that."

He grinned impishly and disappeared below deck.

"He's a great kid," Nick said after a minute. "You're a good mother. No child could ask for more."

Except maybe a father, Stephanie silently added. His words warmed her, and she felt tears prick the backs of her eyes. She hadn't expected Nick's approval. She'd always had the vague feeling that he somehow faulted her for Jason's troubles. "I couldn't ask for a better child," she agreed. "Or one that I could love any more than Jason."

"Do you ever wonder about his father?"

The question came from out in left field. "How do you mean?" Stephanie asked guardedly.

He lifted a shoulder. "I don't know. Why he donated sperm?" His gaze returned to search her face. "Who he is?"

Nick's eyes were dark and unreadable now, Stephanie noticed, but she felt a renewed tension in him. "I've wondered how a man could anonymously donate his sperm to a clinic and then simply walk away. How he could give up that precious part of himself, never knowing what he might've helped create. Of course," she added, smiling softly, "if not for his generosity, I wouldn't have Jason."

Nick had never figured that what he'd done could be viewed as generous. He'd done it for Sally, true. But also for himself, he had to admit. The idea that Stephanie considered the act generous gave the situation a whole new perspective—and him a spark of hope.

Tell her, the warning voice inside Nick's head ordered. Stephanie was giving him everything, opening up all her deepest secrets to him—just as she'd opened her body to him when they'd made love. He couldn't continue withholding the truth from her. It was a potential emotional grenade, armed and ready to detonate without warning in his face—in her face.

"Have you ever thought..." Nick began, then stopped, trying to control his accelerating pulse rate. "Have you ever considered trying to find Jason's father?"

His offhand question sent a ripple of apprehension down Stephanie's spine. She rose to her feet in one jerky movement. "Absolutely not," she stated unequivocally. The gentle sway of the boat almost caused her to lose her footing before she'd fully gained it. "Why would I want to do that?"

She didn't suggest to Nick that maybe Jason's father didn't like kids. Or that maybe he was someone she wouldn't want her child to associate with. She had difficulty imagining that to be the case, though, since she was certain only someone very special could have fathered a child as precious as Jason.

She didn't tell Nick that she feared Jason's father might want to become involved in his son's life. That she feared he wouldn't approve of the way she was raising Jason, that he might try to take him away from her.

"No," she repeated, struggling to rein in her runaway thoughts. "I have no desire to know Jason's biological father."

Nick felt as if a giant fist had crushed the last hope within him, leaving only pain in its wake. She didn't mind some stranger coming into her son's life for a few weeks, maybe even a few months. But she wasn't prepared for someone on a permanent basis, someone who might also have rights. He slowly got to his feet, concealing the raw anguish filling his chest.

Stephanie stood rigidly, her arms wrapped snugly around her thin waist, panic etched on her face. Seeing her distress displaced some of Nick's own sense of loss. "Hey, don't get upset," he said soothingly. "It was just a thought."

Why those five words should contain such terrible sadness, Stephanie couldn't comprehend. But instinctively she reached out to Nick, placing her hand against his chest, trying to give him comfort. She felt the heavy rhythm of his heart even through the thickness of his life jacket. "Thank you."

"For what? Seems I've spent the better part of the last hour saying things that upset you." He hesitated. "Or prying where I shouldn't."

"Oh, I don't know," Stephanie said, smiling up at him. "You're pretty good at saying the right thing at the right time." His gaze roamed over her face, finally coming to rest on her mouth. She felt as if he'd touched her with a white-hot brand.

"The family's getting together week after next for their usual Labor Day blowout. Would you and Jason like to come?"

The invitation surprised Stephanie. "Wouldn't you rather take someone else?"

Nick smiled crookedly. "Who did you have in mind?"

"I don't know. Someone you're serious about?"

"Are you assuming I'm not serious about you?"

Stephanie's breath froze in her lungs and her heart picked up speed. No man had ever looked at her as Nick was right this minute, as if he'd like to devour her. "Do you get together often?" she finally asked, trying to ease the renewed tension between them.

Nick shrugged, still watching her. "Two or three times a year."

"How many people are we talking about here?"

"I lose count from year to year," he said, chuckling.

His laugh had a decidedly sexy ring to it, Stephanie thought. "I always wanted a large family. I particularly wanted lots of children," she said, and was surprised to see some of the laughter leave his eyes.

Nick didn't like to hear the longing in her words. Yeah, he could understand her feelings. "There's a downside to having a large family. Would you like to come and see what it is?" His smile turned wry. "I warn you, it isn't easy to survive one of my family's reunions. You'll be deluged. And some of them don't know the meaning of the word *personal* when it comes to a question."

She found herself wanting very much to meet his family, to get to know this man better, to learn every intimate detail about his life. "I'm certain Jason will love it."

"And what about you? Will you love it?"

"Yes," she told him honestly, the teasing leaving her voice. "But why me? There've got to be scads of women pursuing you. Why me?" she asked again. She watched his eyes darken almost to black.

In that moment Nick wanted to tell her everything. Who he was. How he felt. But he couldn't. She'd just made it clear that she didn't want to know Jason's father. Instead he leaned against the sloping side of the stairway enclosure and pulled Stephanie against him. Opening his legs, he effectively trapped her against himself. "Feel that?" he said huskily, instead of what he really wanted to tell her. "That's one of the best reasons I know." Almost roughly he pushed her away and started down the steps.

Stephanie had always suspected that Nick's remote, detached veneer concealed a dangerous, less-civilized side, a side she wasn't certain was entirely controlled. Watching him now as he steered the sailboat back to port, she was sure she'd been right. Away from shore, his veneer had dropped away, leaving a pirate—a pirate who, she was certain, would take what he wanted without question or permission. She shuddered at the errant thought. Then she smiled, a little whimsically, a little sadly. No matter how hard she tried, she simply couldn't imagine this man being tied down to a wife and family.

He was too much of a loner.

Chapter Twelve

For over two weeks after the day on the sailboat, Stephanie saw Nick only sporadically at the lab and not at all anywhere else. The few times they spoke he was brief and remote, limiting their discussions to updates on the investigation at the lab: There was nothing new to report. As for his other assignment with the agency, well, Matt and he were still waiting. But though he hadn't had a chance to come by to see Jason, Nick talked with him almost daily.

Why he treated her like little more than an acquaintance was a mystery to Stephanie. She sighed. It seemed a bit inappropriate, she chided herself, to be jealous of one's own child.

On the Friday before Labor Day, Nick called to say that he'd be by to pick up Stephanie and Jason at one o'clock Monday to take them to his parents' home. Neither of them heard from him over the weekend, and by Monday morning Stephanie was experiencing a king-size case of the jitters.

Since the day promised to be sweltering, she decided to wear a cool, cotton-knit shirt over a pair of modest white shorts. Nick must have concurred, because he arrived dressed in a pair of shorts so worn the color was no longer discernible, an oversize, blue-striped chambray shirt that had to be one of his favorites and a pair of well-broken-in deck shoes.

He seemed to have reverted to the relaxed man who'd taken them sailing two weeks earlier. He joked with Jason and kept up a running dialogue about swimming, sailing and how many fish they were going to catch the next time they went out in the boat. During the thirty-minute drive to his parents' house, Nick kept sending Stephanie speculative glances, which she found as disconcerting as they were unreadable.

The senior Saxons' home was located in one of the older, tree-lined neighborhoods on the outskirts of D.C. Built in the late thirties, the house had a quiet dignity that was enhanced by its stone construction, slate roof and huge front yard.

His family was everything Nick had told Stephanie, and more. They were indeed numerous and boisterous, and even with her exceptional memory, she abandoned hope of keeping track of everyone's name and who belonged to whom until she'd had a chance to get to know them better.

When they first arrived, Nick stayed protectively close to her, close enough that he could reach over and touch her—which he did frequently. One minute his touch seemed to convey emotional comfort, the next, sensual stimulation. And it definitely kept Stephanie off balance.

Eventually the others separated her from Nick and most of the adults clustered around him. From some of their good-natured teasing, she gathered he wasn't as frequent a visitor as they would like.

Nick's mother walked over to stand beside Stephanie.

"Have you been thoroughly traumatized yet?" Mary asked.

Stephanie laughed and shook her head. "You have a lovely family." She estimated Mary Saxon to be somewhere in her mid- to late-sixties, with a youthful figure and matching outlook on life. Her salt-and-pepper hair accentuated deep brown eyes that sparkled with perception and kindness. When she smiled, Stephanie could see that Nick resembled her.

His family had gone out of their way to make her and Jason feel welcome. The kids, ranging in age from six to thirteen, had corralled Jason as soon as they'd learned he liked computer games and had herded him off to the family room to test his abilities.

"Well, I guess they're a likable bunch, anyway," Mary agreed, smiling. "Why don't you come out to the kitchen and talk with me while I get things together for the cookout?"

As she left the room, Stephanie was aware of Nick's gaze following her. Once in the kitchen, Mary put her to work, gathering what was needed for the meal, and within a few minutes they had finished and were headed out the door.

The backyard was large, easily holding a stone grill and two picnic tables, with plenty of room to spare. The numerous trees ringing the perimeter of the yard filtered out the worst of the sun, and a slight breeze rustled through the leaves.

"You know," Mary commented, setting down the heavily ladened tray she was carrying, "you're the first woman Nick has brought home since Sally died."

"Sally?" Stephanie questioned.

"Nick's wife. She died about eight years ago in a car accident during a freak ice storm." Sadness shadowed Mary's features, then passed.

"I'm sorry." So Nick had been married. She'd somehow known there had to have been someone special in his past. That would explain the haunted look she sometimes saw in his eyes, a look he quickly masked. But Nick had never mentioned anyone and she'd never had the nerve to ask. Eight years ago. That was the winter Stephanie had been trying to get pregnant. She recalled that it had been a particularly bad one for the D.C. area.

"Yes. Everyone misses her." Mary handed Stephanie a couple of tablecloths.

She took them and began spreading one over the nearest table, grateful for something to do.

"She was a wonderful girl, very sweet and compassionate. But she wasn't right for Nick."

Mary's candid remarks threw Stephanie. What was she supposed to say? She busied herself meticulously smoothing out every wrinkle in the second tablecloth, waiting to see what Nick's mother would say next.

"Nick needs someone who will challenge him. Someone who isn't..." she searched for the right word "...*predictable.*" Mary finished setting out eating utensils on the first table. "I imagine you keep Nick on his toes."

"Oh, please don't misunderstand. There's nothing serious between Nick and me," Stephanie felt obligated to explain. *Unless you count the fact that I'm al-*

ready in love with your son. "We were thrown together temporarily because of a problem at my work."

"Whatever you say, dear," Mary said, her warm brown eyes crinkling at the corners. "But you should be warned that everyone here is very curious about you."

Stephanie couldn't help wondering what Mary's disclosures signified. Was it possible that Nick did care for her more than he'd let on? A tenuous hope flared to life. *Don't be foolish,* she warned herself, trying to extinguish it before it caught fire. *Don't set yourself up for unnecessary heartache.* So what if she was the first woman Nick had brought home in years? So what if he'd made breathtaking love to her? He'd never said one word about love or marriage or even a long-term relationship. Still...

At that moment the back door slammed open and several kids came bounding into the yard. Jason followed a few paces behind.

"Guess what, Grandma?" said Sylvia.

Mary gave her thirteen-year-old granddaughter an affectionate look. "I couldn't possibly."

"Jason beat every one of us at Nintendo," the girl said without rancor. "He's bunches of levels ahead of all of us."

"Well, good for him. You kids need to have your wings clipped every now and again." Mary handed her some utensils. "Why don't you finish setting the other table?"

Jason came over to Stephanie. "Are you having a good time?" she asked.

"Yeah." He grinned. "They want me to show them how to move up to the next levels in Nintendo."

"That's nice." Stephanie couldn't have been more pleased for her son. It seemed Jason had been accepted quickly by this group of strangers. She well knew that some kids became very upset when he consistently beat them. Nick had warned her that his family was competitive. And it seemed they weren't about to pass up the opportunity to gain pointers from an expert, once they'd discovered Jason's skill.

Just then Nick loped down the steps leading from the house. Stephanie felt a familiar flutter of excitement when he headed straight for her. He stopped beside Jason, placing a hand on his shoulder, but Jason was absorbed in watching the other kids. Nick stood close enough to Stephanie that she felt the heat radiating from his body.

"Hi," he said to her. "Are you surviving?"

She chuckled, trying to keep her voice even. "Your mother asked me almost the same thing. Is there something I should know about your family?"

Something flickered in his eyes, then was gone.

"Hey, neat!" Jason interrupted. He'd apparently figured out where the other children were headed.

In one corner of the backyard hung an old tire swing, suspended from the limb of an ancient oak tree. It was located in an ideal spot—far enough from the house so the kids wouldn't feel as though they were being spied on, but close enough so that an adult could keep an eye on things. At the moment all the kids were clamoring for a turn on the tire.

"Gotta go, Mom," Jason told her, heading to join them.

"Be careful." Stephanie was none too enthusiastic about Jason participating in this particular activity, but she refrained from commenting.

Before he'd taken a dozen steps, Nick called to him. "Hold on, champ."

The boy looked up questioningly.

"We have some rules everyone has to follow," Nick told him. "Otherwise, you might get hurt."

"You mean things that'll take all the fun out of it," Jason grumbled.

"You may be right," Nick agreed, grinning.

Nick's gaze met Stephanie's over Jason's head and something almost like parental understanding passed between them. It created an odd feeling near her heart.

She smiled to herself as she watched them walk away side by side. Her son could seldom pass up a new challenge, in fact he seemed to thrive on them. And he wasn't any too thrilled with restrictions. It seemed he had several traits in common with Nick, not to mention the Saxon family.

Several more adults straggled out of the house, and Mary commandeered her husband, Frank, and James, one of Nick's younger brothers, to take over grilling hamburgers.

A few minutes later the older of Nick's two sisters came over to Stephanie. Louise was a younger version of Mary. "Nick seems to really enjoy your son," she said.

Stephanie chuckled. "The feeling's mutual, except Jason goes a little further. He plain worships Nick."

"Jason's a great kid," Louise continued. "Fits right in."

"Thank you," Stephanie said, pleased that she agreed. Jason had been a little overwhelmed at first, but the younger kids seemed to accept him because of his age, the older ones because of his maturity. This was just the kind of family Stephanie had always longed for, had dreamed of one day having for Jason. And herself.

"It's good to see Nick interested in someone with a child. He's so good with children, he should have a houseful." Shaking her head sadly, Louise added, "Maybe if Sally hadn't died so suddenly..."

Stephanie made a sympathetic sound. She could easily imagine how empty her own life would be without Jason.

It was obvious that Nick cared deeply for his large family. He adored his nieces and nephews, easily tolerating their teasing and roughhousing. But he seemed to hold himself apart, almost as if he were an observer rather than a member. Stephanie couldn't quite put her finger on the cause. At certain moments, when she was sure he thought no one was watching, she caught glimpses of wistfulness in his eyes, almost a yearning. It made her want to go to him and wipe away whatever was causing him pain.

"Sally was a love, but she wasn't right for Nick. He needs someone who stimulates him intellectually." Louise looked over at her and winked. "I have a feeling you do that very well."

Stephanie felt a blush climb her cheeks. Louise had made the same comment as Mary. It warmed her to know that Nick's family seemed to approve of her, but how should she respond? she wondered. She was saved from answering when she saw Nick heading back toward her. As soon as he reached her, he casually draped an arm around her shoulders. Stephanie's heart did a crazy little flip-flop.

"Well, I'll leave you two," Louise said. "Stay here and be grateful for the solitude while you can."

"Still enjoying yourself?" he asked in a low voice, studying her face.

"I'm having a wonderful time." She looked up at him, smiling into his dark eyes. "I didn't realize you'd been married before."

He smiled wryly, but a trace of sadness shadowed his eyes. "I see they didn't waste any time filling you in on the family history."

"I'm sorry. I shouldn't have mentioned it."

"It was a long time ago." He looked over at the kids, still playing with the old swing. "We'd known each other since we were kids. She'd written faithfully while I was in Nam. It had been a vital link to home. When I got back, she was here, waiting."

Though it was clear to Stephanie that Sally's death pained him, Nick sounded as if he were talking about a sister, not his wife. Where was the passion she'd glimpsed in him, had in fact experienced with him?

"Everybody loved Sally." He lifted a shoulder. "It seemed natural for us to get married."

"And you never had any children."

"She was killed before we had the chance." His jaw tightened and something raw and anguished came and went in his eyes.

He'd wanted children, Stephanie knew intuitively. "I'm sorry," she said again.

He glanced down at her. "It was a long time ago." He couldn't very well tell her that Sally had always been more friend than lover. His feeling for his wife certainly hadn't approached what he felt for this woman standing beside him. Nor had what he'd experienced with any other woman approached it. He'd experienced lust before, but nothing like what he felt for Stephanie. This went far beyond mere carnal craving. What he felt for Stephanie touched his very soul.

She was giving him another opening to tell her. But could he risk telling her the truth? *Should* he risk it? Their conversation on the boat had shown him clearly how badly she'd wanted to have a child. Jason. His son. Would she settle for a sterile husband? How could he ask to become a part of her life when he had nothing more to offer her?

But he wanted to. God, how he wanted to!

He'd deliberately stayed away from Stephanie as much as possible since the day on his boat. He'd needed some space to come to terms with the jumble of emotions about this whole difficult situation regarding Jason. One thing he'd discovered early—he'd missed Stephanie.

The rest of the family began straggling out of the house, demanding food. Mary, completely unruffled by their demands, gave each of them some task to hurry the preparations along. Finally she called, "Come and get it," and close to twenty people scrambled for a place at one of the tables.

Stephanie slid onto one end of a bench, moving over slightly when Nick slid in beside her. The bench was crowded, which meant that there was little room between them. His left thigh, covered with a smattering of dark hair, was pressed intimately against her own. It made concentrating on her hamburger extremely difficult.

The meal was pleasantly chaotic, with everyone vying to put their two cents' worth into every ongoing conversation. An important detail Nick had failed to mention about his family, Stephanie reflected, was that they were warm and loving. And accepting. This group enjoyed spirited debates on topics ranging from politics to religion, and no one batted an eye when Stephanie contributed her opinions with just as much enthusiasm.

The kids were the first to finish eating, and one by one headed back to the swing. Stephanie absently watched Jason climb onto the old tire when it was his turn. He pumped his sturdy swimmer's legs harder and harder, and the swing climbed higher and higher. When he'd gotten it going at a good pace, he grabbed hold of the rope with both hands and worked first one foot, then the other under him until he was standing. The other kids yelled and waved at him. Grinning broadly, Jason let go of the rope with his left hand to wave back.

The swing had reached the peak of its next upward climb, about six or seven feet in the air, when Jason's foot slipped. Horrified, Stephanie watched as Jason, in what seemed like slow motion, struggled to regain his balance. His right hand grabbed for the rope, but it was too late.

He hit the ground with a dull, sickening thud.

Hemmed in on both sides, Stephanie tried to work her legs free of the picnic table so she could get to her son. But Nick was way ahead of her. Within seconds he was off the bench and kneeling beside Jason. The boy, lying on his back, was very still. Cold fear slithered through Stephanie.

As she approached, Nick glanced up at her. "He's all right," he assured her.

It had been the briefest of eye contact, but Stephanie hadn't missed the fear, and something else, darkening his eyes. It took her several heartbeats to identify what she'd witnessed.

Nick Saxon loved her child.

"Just got the breath knocked out of him," he said, helping Jason sit up. Nick gently held him while he sucked in the first painful breath, refilling his lungs.

"Thank God," Stephanie said, kneeling beside them and rubbing her son's back comfortingly. Jason didn't cry. He didn't say anything, either. And he didn't leave Nick's arms in favor of his mother's.

Stephanie became aware that everyone had gathered around them, all talking at once. Even though Jason was okay, the whole family was visibly shaken, especially the kids. They were quiet now, their voices subdued. The last thing she wanted was them blaming themselves for what had happened.

"Come on, kids," Stephanie said, standing and starting toward an open space in the yard. "Let's see how good you are at telling stories."

She settled the youngsters in a circle and started a story about a boy and girl who traveled the galaxy with their parents, discovering strange new worlds and meeting many interesting life-forms. Each child had to begin where the last one left off. Within minutes, the children had forgotten the recent trauma and were absorbed in weaving an adventure for their new, imaginary friends. After a while, Jason came over and sat down next to Stephanie, leaning against her arm.

But nothing could erase from Stephanie's memory the look she'd witnessed in Nick's eyes.

On the drive back Jason fell asleep in the car with his head in Stephanie's lap. Once they reached home, Nick carried the exhausted child inside and up to his room. He was so tired he didn't have the energy to undress himself. Without waiting to be asked, Nick helped Stephanie get Jason into his pajamas and tucked into bed. They were almost out of the room when Jason spoke.

"I had fun today, Nick," he said sleepily. "Your family's neat."

Nick walked back over to the bed and smiled down at him. "I'm glad you enjoyed yourself, sport. Go back to sleep."

"'Kay. Nick?"

"Yeah?"

"Thanks for taking care of me tonight."

"You're welcome," Nick said, leaning over to ruffle the boy's hair.

"Nick?"

"Hmm?"

"I'm sorry I broke your rules about the swing."

Nick settled on the edge of the bed beside Jason. "We're just glad you didn't get seriously hurt."

"Thanks for not yelling at me."

Nick grinned. "Did you expect me to?"

Jason thought about that. "Well, my friends' dads do. A lot."

"They do, do they?" Nick straightened the covers over the boy's small frame. "And do you think they have a good reason to?"

Jason sighed heavily. "I guess. If I promise I won't break any more rules, will you take me back to visit your family again?"

There was a knot in Nick's throat that he wasn't certain he could speak around. "Any time you want to and your mom will let you."

"Great," Jason said sleepily. He was quiet for a while. "It was pretty dumb of me to stand up on that swing, huh?"

"Not dumb, but certainly not smart. Why did you do it?"

Jason glanced up at Nick, then down at the corner of the spread he was fiddling with. "I guess I was showing off," he admitted sheepishly.

His childish honesty surprised Nick, and he felt a swell of pride that his son had so much insight. There were a few adults in Nick's experience who could take a lesson from Jason. "You don't have to prove yourself to anyone." He squeezed the boy's shoulder. "All you have to do is be yourself. If you're sincere, people will accept you just the way you are. You understand?"

Nodding solemnly, Jason sat up and threw himself at Nick. "I love you," he said, his voice muffled against the man's shoulder.

As he enfolded Jason in a fierce hug, Nick's breath lodged somewhere in his chest and he thought his heart was going to explode. It took him several seconds before he could speak in what he hoped was a normal voice. "I love you too, Son."

Stephanie felt the sting of tears and slipped out of the room before Nick could realize she'd witnessed the private moment between them.

He found her waiting for him at the bottom of the stairs. She looked seductively tousled and a little sleepy herself. And he knew he was too emotionally raw to resist her. He stopped a foot away.

Stephanie could feel the heat from his body. Her hand fluttered to her throat and then dropped to her side. "Can I get you something?"

Nick cursed silently. It didn't look like he was going to get a break tonight. He knew it was a perfectly innocent question. But he had the almost overwhelming urge to tell her bluntly, and in intimate detail, that, hell yes, she could get him something—her, alone, naked in his bed, for several days. No, make that weeks.

No, make that for the rest of his life.

He closed the distance between them and slid his hands into her thick hair. "I'd like something." Without asking permission, he lowered his mouth to hers. And just as she had before, she responded wholeheartedly. He shouldn't kiss her, Nick told himself. But her innocent question had turned him on in ways the most seductive sex siren never could. Hell, he'd made love to her once. Surely he could restrain his lust until he summoned the courage to tell her what she had to know.

It took all the strength he could muster to lift his mouth away from hers. He closed his eyes and rested his forehead against hers. "Will you go out with me?"

She leaned back to look up at him. "Are you asking me out on a date?"

"You could call it that," he said wryly.

She smiled and drew his head back to hers. He didn't consider resisting.

"This," Nick told her between sexy little nibbles of her lower lip, "isn't why I'm asking you out." He felt her lips curve into another smile.

"No?"

He kissed her again. This time harder and with urgency. "Absolutely not." He seemed to be speaking more to himself than to her. "I should never have made love to you in the first place."

She was too aware of his arousal pressing against her stomach to take his disclaimer seriously, or be hurt by it, "Why not?" she asked without artifice, her voice sounding high and shallow.

"I rushed you. You weren't ready for it."

"Did you hear me complaining?"

Nick noticed that Stephanie's smile held a hint of Jason's subtle mischievousness. The thought hit him somewhere in the region of his gut. When had he stopped looking for Jason's resemblance to himself and begun searching for traces of her?

He groaned. "Stephanie, don't. I'm trying to do the right thing here."

"The right thing." She slid her arms around his neck. "What do you have in mind?"

His chuckle was strained. Her guileless teasing was like an aphrodisiac. But he couldn't allow himself to respond. Not when something so vital was still unresolved between them. And, damn it, he wanted it resolved. He prayed to whatever benevolence there was in the universe that, once it *was* resolved, Stephanie would still welcome him anywhere near her or his son. "I need to talk to you," he said, his tone serious. "Preferably someplace where we won't be interrupted."

Making love to her that first time, he now realized, had merely served to whet his appetite. The first time had been too frantic and over too damned quick. Right this minute he wanted to run his hands slowly up under her thin cotton shirt—that shirt that had tantalized him all afternoon because he knew damned well what it just barely concealed—and stroke her soft, full breasts. And when he'd made them peak into hard pebbles, he wanted to take one, then the other into his mouth and soothe it. Then he wanted to spend hours exploring every delicious inch of her. And when they were both out of their minds with wanting, he would lay her down and make love to her again and again and again....

Stephanie sobered. "All right. When?"

Nick sighed in frustration, disturbingly aware that his time wasn't his own until he'd stamped Finished on this last assignment with the agency. But he couldn't afford to wait that long to tell her. He had no way of knowing how much more time this assignment might take. He'd simply have to take a chance that, this once, fate would deal him a lucky hand and give him one more uninterrupted day to tell Stephanie everything. "Tomorrow night?"

She nodded. "Where are you taking me?"

"How about dinner at my place?"

Her smile was innocently provocative. "That sounds . . . interesting."

Don't tempt me, he wanted to tell her. Instead he said, "I'll pick you up around six."

He looked as if he'd like to kiss her again, Stephanie thought, but he didn't. And she felt an aching loss.

Maybe there was a chance, Nick told himself as he drove away from Stephanie's house. She'd obviously liked his family, and they had accepted her affectionately into their midst. She'd been a hit with the kids. Maybe he did have something to offer her. Maybe Stephanie would accept his large, still-growing family as a substitute for more children of her own.

He was tired of feeling like a fraud, acting like a coward. He owed her the truth. All of it. She'd told him everything about herself, never pulling any punches. But he was forced to admit that he was just plain scared. He didn't even want to consider what it would do to her when he told her.

Anytime now Matt could call to tell him this last undercover assignment was about to go down. It could be dangerous. It was possible Nick might die before ever having told Stephanie the truth. And if he was going to die, he at least wanted his son to know who his father was.

Nick rolled down the car window and let the cool night breeze wash over him.

Who was he trying to fool? He just plain couldn't wait any longer for her. He loved Stephanie, he finally admitted. And he had to find out if there was a chance, any chance at all, to build a life with her and Jason.

"You know," Alex said, seconds after Nick had walked out the door, "a fire extinguisher in this entrance hall might not be such a bad idea."

Hand over her heart, Stephanie swung around to face her sister. "You nearly gave me a coronary," she scolded.

"Hey, any heart attacks being given out tonight aren't by me."

Stephanie felt her face flame. "I didn't know you were home."

"I just got in. I came in through the garage."

Not that she'd have noticed, Stephanie reflected with self-mockery, if Alex had come through the front door and walked right over her and Nick.

"Want a cup of herbal tea before we go up?" Alex asked, heading down the hall.

"Why not?" she said, following. She probably wouldn't be able to sleep much tonight, anyway.

"Something bothering you?" Alex glanced at Stephanie as they entered the kitchen. "I mean besides the fact that you're hot and bothered."

Stephanie shook her head and chuckled. "Leave it to you to get right to the point." She took down the tea and two mugs. "I'm just wondering if I might have made a mistake tonight."

"What kind of mistake are we talking about here?"

"Agreeing to go out with Nick."

"Ah." Alex grew serious. "You want this guy?" She filled a container with water and set it in the microwave oven.

Stephanie was quiet for several seconds. "Yes," she finally said, a little surprised at her own vehemence.

"Then go get him, Sis."

A smile played at the corners of her mouth. "You think I can, huh?"

"Damn straight." Alex laughed out loud. It was a full-throated laugh, a laugh Stephanie had watched her sister use on more than one man to bring him to his knees. "Besides, if you want him badly enough, what other choice do you have?"

What, indeed? Stephanie thought. Weeks ago Nick had said almost the same thing when he'd challenged her to push aside her fear and let him teach her to swim. She smiled, wondering if he was prepared to have his own advice used against him.

Chapter Thirteen

The moment Stephanie opened the front door the next evening, Nick realized he'd vastly overestimated his self-control where she was concerned. She was wearing a deceptively modest red dress that skimmed her figure, but accentuated all the right places. He'd never seen her in red before; she usually preferred more subdued colors. Tonight he found that either the dress or its color, or maybe both, were doing bewitching things to her hair, her skin, her eyes.

"Hello," he said aloud, his voice husky.

Stephanie smiled beguilingly. "Hi."

He searched for a distraction. "Where's Jason?"

"Alex took him for ice cream. They should be back any minute now. You want to come in and wait?" She stepped back, opening the door wider, inviting him in.

"No, I'll catch him later," he said, glancing at his watch. "It's a long drive to the house. Ready to go?"

"All right. Let me get my things."

In the car Stephanie sat angled toward him, one foot tucked under her, her left arm propped on the back of the seat. The casual position presented Nick with a tantalizing glimpse of a smooth thigh—much more than he felt capable of handling tonight. She said little and seemed a bit preoccupied. While she hummed softly along with the tune coming from the CD player, she kept playing enticingly with a loose strand of her hair.

He tried to concentrate on driving, but his gaze kept straying back to her. The evening air, unusually warm for September, whipped through the open windows, tossing a lock of hair across her smooth right cheek. The urge to reach over and tuck it behind her ear surprised him. He gripped the steering wheel tighter.

He'd asked her out so they could talk, Nick reminded himself grimly, not make love. Which was what he wanted to do. And he doubted she'd be receptive to that idea once he got through telling her what he had to. The knot of apprehension in his stomach grew heavier and he experienced a bitter sense of impending loss.

Once he got them home and out of the close confines of the Jeep, Nick hoped he'd have better control over himself, over the situation. But it didn't get easier. Stephanie insisted on helping him with the simple meal of grilled chicken, baked potatoes and tossed salads. She seemed always just within touching distance. And she smelled of some exotic fragrance that he was certain couldn't be manmade.

Her close proximity in what he'd always considered a good-size kitchen was shredding his tenuous resolve. He wanted to touch her. He wanted to forget what he knew he had to tell her. He wanted to take her upstairs to his bed and make love to her over and over until she wouldn't give a damn who he was or that for weeks he'd kept something so vital from her.

He poured them each a glass of white zinfandel, and they sat down to eat at the small table in the kitchen. Conversation was sporadic. Once the table was cleared and the few dishes rinsed and loaded in the dishwasher, Stephanie dried her hands.

"Do you realize," she said carefully, picking up her glass of wine and holding it with both hands, "you've never shown me all of your house?" Her sometimes frosty, tawny green eyes had warmed to burnished gold. They sparkled with humor, and something else. "I've often wondered exactly what you're hiding in all these rooms."

She'd know one secret soon enough, he thought bleakly. While his conscience mocked him as a coward, he grabbed at a final chance to postpone the inevitable. "Let's see if I can put that suspicion to rest." He held out his hand to her.

He led her through several rooms, explaining a little about how he'd fixed up each one. And Stephanie seemed enthralled with every detail. He found her interest oddly gratifying.

"I loved this house the first time I saw it," she told him. "It's warm and inviting. Exactly the kind I've always dreamed of living in."

They had stopped outside the master bedroom. Nick reached inside the doorway and flipped the light switch, then let Stephanie enter ahead of him. The bedside lamp gave off a muted glow, wrapping the room in intimacy. Propping a shoulder against the doorframe, he watched her explore, not certain he was ready to see her here.

He'd bought the small farm and house after Sally's death as a means to heal himself, a means to create something that would be uniquely his. Something that might compensate for what he'd lost.

He'd furnished this room for himself, for his tastes, his comfort. It was his refuge. The bed was large to accommodate his size. Yet he could easily envision Stephanie in it. He'd chosen masculine colors of deep browns and rich golds for the carpet and bedding. Yet she looked right at home, as if he'd instinctively chosen them just for her.

She investigated the master bath with its oversize fixtures, poked her head inside the huge walk-in closet, checked out the view from the two large windows in the room, then came to a stop beside his bed, still holding her glass of wine. She took a sip and stood there several moments running her free hand slowly back and forth over the soft brown comforter.

Nick groaned silently as erotic images began forming in his mind, sending overheated blood to the lower region of his anatomy. He needed to get Stephanie back downstairs to neutral territory or no way in hell were they going to do much talking. At least not about what he'd brought her here to discuss. The only words left in his mind were provocative and sexy.

Stephanie took a deep breath, wondering if she had the nerve to go through with this. But she'd made up her mind, for once in her life she was going to tempt fate. She'd spent hours thinking about Nick and their relationship. And she'd decided that his feeling for her had to run much deeper than he was letting on.

A man couldn't be as patient, sympathetic and understanding as he had been with her and Jason without caring. Last night Nick had confirmed that he loved her son. That gave her hope.

The bed was a plain, pencil-post frame. Very stark. Very masculine. Very sensual. She looked across the room to where Nick still leaned against the doorjamb, his unreadable dark gaze burning into her. Vivid memories of Nick's lovemaking crowded out all else, leaving in their wake a heated pool of arousal deep inside. He couldn't have been that passionate, that considerate a lover, she reasoned, if he didn't care for her just a little.

"This bed gives me several ideas for a fantasy."

Nick didn't move, but a corner of his mouth lifted in a wry smile. "Another fairy tale?" he asked, remembering in erotic detail the outcome of the last one.

The strained note in his voice boosted her confidence. "Oh no," she said softly setting down her glass on the nightstand. "This is going to be hard, hot fact." She began walking toward him.

No, not walking, Nick corrected; her seductive movements were more like gliding. He swallowed, his body instantly responding. This was a side of Stephanie he'd never seen. He straightened away from the doorframe, wondering if she had any idea what she was toying with. "Stephanie, we need to talk."

She stopped in front of him. "All right," she said provocatively, "let's talk." She placed her hand against his chest, right over his heart, and found its erratic beat encouraging. "Do you want me?"

He made a guttural sound that could have been a laugh and looked down at himself. "I think that's obvious."

"Oh," she said, leaning into the hard length of him, sliding her arms around his neck. "I'd begun to wonder."

"We need to talk," he repeated in a strangled voice.

"Sometimes the best communication isn't verbal," she whispered just before she drew his mouth down to hers.

Why was he fighting her? he wondered, as he felt himself going down for the count. She wanted him. He sure as hell wanted her. And this might very well be the last time he would have her. Why not take tonight to show her in intimate detail just how much he loved her? After she knew the truth, there was no reason to hope she'd want anything else to do with him.

As soon as their mouths touched, Nick deepened the kiss, trying to communicate just how much she affected him...just how much he wanted her...just how much she meant to him.

He slid both hands into her hair, taking his time, gently slanting his lips over hers, exploring her mouth leisurely, thoroughly. When he finally lifted his head, Stephanie released a breathless sigh.

"I'm not certain," she said, her voice unsteady, "I know what to do next."

Amusement along with arousal glittered in his eyes. "Then you *are* trying to seduce me?"

She chuckled, the sound a sensual rasp. "If you have to ask, I must not be doing it right."

Nick instantly sobered. She couldn't possibly know how much her sweet seduction meant to him. "Ah, honey, believe me, you couldn't do it any better if you practiced for a lifetime." In one smooth motion, he lifted her into his arms and carried her over to his bed. Slowly setting her feet on the floor, he kept her body in intimate contact with his. He shuddered, and he wondered if he had a prayer of hanging onto his sanity long enough to make this right for her.

Stephanie sensed an element of desperation in Nick. It was as if he were imprinting her on his memory, she thought dimly.

And he was. Nick wanted to know all of her, each taste, each smell, each texture. He wanted to hear every sexy sound she made while in the throes of passion. He wanted every memory he could create tonight.

Unzipping the back of her dress, he pushed it off her shoulders and down over her hips. He took scant notice of what she had on underneath. He had the impression of something silky and red and much sexier than it needed to be—and he wanted it gone. So he could see *her,* feel *her.*

With unsteady hands he peeled away the flimsy material. Her only other garment was a scrap of red silk that passed for panties. His breath lodged in his lungs. In the muted light of the bedside lamp, her skin seemed to glow. Cupping her breasts in his hands, he brought the nipples to stiff peaks with his thumbs.

A distant corner of his mind recognized that she'd planned this seduction well. He'd have to tell her sometime when he was saner that none of this was necessary—that if she were wearing nothing but rags he'd still find her a temptation he couldn't resist.

"Nick," Stephanie pleaded. She tried to unbutton his shirt, but he stopped her.

"Slowly." He knew if he let her undress him, this would be over before it started. "I want to savor this," he told her, his voice barely recognizable, "savor all of you."

And then he replaced his hands with his mouth.

Stephanie sucked in a sharp breath and moaned, the sound coming from deep within her. When her legs gave way, Nick laid her back against the thick comforter, stretching out beside her. The rough texture of his clothing softly abrading her bare skin was unbearably erotic. The weight of Nick pressing against her intensified Stephanie's craving to pull him closer.

But Nick wouldn't let her. He captured her hands in one of his, anchoring them above her head. He gently ran his free hand teasingly across each breast, then down her stomach until he reached her panties. With infinite care, he removed them. Completely bare now, Stephanie looked up at him, her eyes shimmering with a mixture of desire and trust. He swallowed and moved his hand over the soft curls hiding the core of her, teasing, but never quite satisfying.

Stephanie shifted restlessly against his hand and moaned. With a harsh sound, he released her hands and stood to finally strip out of his own clothes. As soon as he was beside her again he covered her mouth with his, trying to convey wordlessly how immeasurably desirable she was to him. How much he needed her.

He moved his mouth to her breasts, sweetly tormenting each one. He kissed his way down to her stomach, savoring the smooth skin. Then lower still. When she was half out of her mind with need, when she was breathless and writhing and moaning his name, Nick moved over her.

This time when Stephanie reached to pull him to her, Nick had no resistance left.

She was hot and tight, and nothing had ever felt so right to Nick. He struggled to slow the pace, to prolong the exquisite pleasure, the feeling of being complete, but when he felt Stephanie contract around him, he was lost. He groaned against the inevitable, then gave himself up to it.

"I love you...."

I love you. In a distant corner of her heart, before the waves of pleasure took her under, Stephanie thought how perfect it would be if she were to conceive from their lovemaking tonight.

For a long while neither of them moved, both lying where they'd collapsed earlier. Finally Nick stirred.

Stephanie noticed a renewed tension in him. She raised up on one elbow and looked down at him in the dim light. "Nick?" she said softly. "What's wrong?"

He pulled her against him and gave her a hard kiss. "I love you."

Stephanie's heart tripped over itself. "So I didn't imagine it." She smiled, nuzzling his chest.

His answering smile was strained. "No, you didn't imagine it."

"I love you, too," she whispered.

His arm flexed around her, and he was quiet for several long seconds. "When two people say they love each other, that usually means they'll get married."

"Usually," Stephanie agreed, holding her breath.

"And have children."

"I'd like another child." She could feel the rigid set of his muscles.

"I want you to marry me." He pressed a finger against her lips. "But there's something else you need to know before you give me an answer."

Stephanie waited.

Finally he took in a deep breath, then let it out. "I'm sterile."

Her heart ached at the loss, for him, for her. She thought of her earlier hope tonight that she might conceive from their lovemaking. "I'm sorry." The arm

Nick was using to hold her close tightened almost painfully. "Is there anything that can be done?"

He shook his head. "Nothing. Believe me, Sally and I tried everything...." He let the words trail off. He wasn't ready yet to tell her all of it. "It's complete and it's permanent."

"How?" she asked, starting to raise her head so she could look at him. But he held her firmly, almost as if he were afraid to let her go.

"The doctors at the fertility clinic said something about a bad infection I had while I was a POW." He shrugged one powerful shoulder. "I don't think they really know for sure."

Stephanie's hand sought out the faint scar on his left shoulder, and she traced it lightly with one finger. The similarity between their lives was ironic, she reflected. Having been threatened with possible sterility, she could well understand how devastating it must have been for Nick to learn that he would never be a father. She couldn't imagine a life without Jason. She wished Nick had been as fortunate.

It had taken a lot for him to tell her this. She knew that some men considered sterility a slur to their manhood. And she could well understand the reason for Nick's reluctance to make love to her again. He must have felt he didn't have the right until he'd told her the truth about himself, about his sterility. His sense of honesty touched her.

"Oh, Nick," she whispered, tears threatening, "I love you." She lifted her head so she could kiss him, a sweet kiss conveying all the emotions welling up inside her. "You've done so much for me. And for Jason." She didn't say aloud that his most precious gift to her was making her feel that he wanted her just for herself, not for some ulterior motive.

Something like pain flickered in his eyes. "Is that what this is all about?" he asked, his tone neutral. "You're repaying what you think you owe me?"

A slight frown pleated her forehead. "Of course not. Why—"

"Don't be too quick," he interrupted, smiling grimly. "There's still one more thing I haven't told you."

The jarring ring of the phone cut off his words. He cursed softly and rolled over to snatch up the receiver.

The conversation was brief and to the point. Seconds later, Nick hung up. "That was Matt. I have to go." He left the bed and went to the closet.

When he was dressed in a dark shirt and slacks, he came back to the bed and looked down at her. And silently cursed fate. There wasn't time to tell her the rest of it. Not when he had to leave immediately, not when he might not be back for who knew how long, not when he couldn't be here to repair the damage.

"Will you wait for me?" He knew it was an unreasonable request. He had no idea how long this might take. But he needed her promise—something he could hang on to, something that said this wouldn't be the end, that there was hope for a future with her and Jason.

The jumble of emotions Stephanie glimpsed in Nick's eyes disturbed her. She wanted nothing more than to reassure him. She caught his hand in hers and brought it to her lips. "I'll stay as long as I can," she promised against his palm.

Some of the tension eased from Nick. "Thank you." He leaned down and gave her a hard kiss. "Make yourself at home." He kissed her again, this time longer, hotter. "I don't know how long this will take, but I'll get word to you as soon as I can—if I can."

Stephanie started to get up to see him out, but he held her still. "No. Stay where you are." He wanted to carry the image of her waiting for him in his bed. "I love you. Promise me you won't forget that."

"Be careful." Stephanie pulled his mouth to hers and kissed him.

It took almost more willpower than Nick had to pull away and walk out the door.

After Nick left, Stephanie lay in bed, remembering his last words. *I love you. Promise me you won't forget that.* How could she? She loved him. Body and soul.

The bed was too empty without Nick in it. To fill the time until he returned, she decided to get up and dress, then explore the few areas he hadn't gotten a chance to show her. She smiled remembering the reason why.

She was going to love living here. And so would Jason. Nick would make a wonderful father. He loved Jason. And Jason certainly loved him.

One of the rooms they hadn't gotten around to was Nick's office. There was something very revealing, she reflected, about an office in the home. It was far more personal, more intimate, than one located where strangers might have access to it.

Nick's was in a corner bedroom and was sparsely furnished in the same masculine colors and sizes as the rest of the house. There was a bookcase containing a hodgepodge of reference manuals and several framed photos of his family, many of whom she'd met yesterday. Along one wall was a long table where he kept a fax machine, copier, printer and two phones. A large desk with a state-of-the-art computer on one corner took up the center of the room. The only chair sat behind the desk. Stephanie smiled wryly. When Nick came into this office, he obviously intended to work.

She walked over to take a closer look at the computer. As she sat down, she noticed a folder lying beside it. It was the only other item on the desk, which was surprising. Since she knew Nick was involved in at least two ongoing assignments, she would have expected several files and numerous papers. She would have disregarded this one, but Nick's distinctive handwriting on the outside caught her eye.

He'd written her name.

A small warning voice told her to leave it alone. It was none of her business. But why would Nick have a folder with her name on it? Maybe it had something to do with his investigation at the lab, she told herself, trying to still her growing uneasiness.

Almost as if someone were directing her, she opened the folder. It contained page after page of information about her, ranging from public to private. Mechanically, Stephanie turned the pages. As she read, one part of her mind kept telling her she was invading Nick's privacy, while another part kept asking why he should have all this data on her. It covered almost her entire life.

Her apprehension grew in small, painful increments. But it wasn't until she'd read the final sheet that the full significance of the folder hit her. Jason's name was printed at the top, followed by numerous details about his short life. Including the fact that he had been conceived by artificial insemination. Across the bottom, scrawled in Nick's almost illegible handwriting, was one cryptic message.

Jason Harcourt . . . my son.

All the events of the past several weeks came flooding back with the force of a tidal wave. Everything else fell in its wake, leaving nothing inside Stephanie but a hollow feeling of dread.

The sense of betrayal almost stopped her heart. Almost, but not quite. Otherwise she wouldn't be feeling this crushing pain.

Stephanie shoved the folder away from her as if it were something vile, scattering the pages across the desk and onto the floor.

She thought she'd known betrayal before—when she'd discovered her first and, until Nick, only lover had been eager to use her mind, preferably without having to use her body. When she'd discovered time after time that people weren't interested in her, but in exploiting her talents. But nothing, nothing, came close to this.

Abruptly she stood, rubbing her arms against the chill invading her. She walked over to a window and stared into the blackness. Think clearly, she silently ordered herself, striving for calm. What did this mean? To her? To Jason?

Was she jumping to conclusions? Was she misinterpreting the evidence? But Nick's words of earlier this evening returned to taunt her. *The doctors at the fertility clinic... Believe me, Sally and I tried everything....*

No, she wasn't jumping to conclusions.

Why had Nick kept the fact that he was Jason's father from her? Particularly when he'd had so many opportunities to tell her?

Like that first day in the lab, when she'd asked him if he had children. What had he said? Her photographic memory ruthlessly supplied the answer: *"No one calls me Dad."*

Later that same afternoon he'd asked if Jason had a father helping him. Nick had already known, damn him. *He'd already known the answer.*

Of course, he'd had a very good reason not to tell her. He was *sterile*. The word kept echoing in her head like a funeral dirge.

Jason would be his only child. And Nick loved his son.

What did he want? She'd seen his relentless determination in accomplishing whatever he'd set out to do, whether gaining her cooperation in the lab investigation, making certain his partner returned safely or charming his way into her private life. And Jason's.

She recalled how determined Nick had been to finish this last assignment for the agency. Not just because his partner needed him, but because Nick never left something unfinished. Stephanie shuddered. What did that mean for Jason?

Wouldn't Nick be even more ruthless when it came to his son?

Oh God, just like so many others, Nicholas Saxon wanted something from her. *Her son.*

She felt nausea rise in her throat. She couldn't trust him—should never have trusted him. She couldn't believe anything he'd said to her. *Of course* Nick had told her he loved her. *Of course* he'd asked her to marry him. He'd probably say anything, do anything, to keep his only child.

Something cold slid through her, freezing her heart, her hopes, her newfound happiness. For the moment even the pain was frozen, leaving only emptiness in its place.

But, a little voice whispered, *he loves Jason*. If the situation were reversed, to what lengths would *she* go?

Stephanie pushed the thought away. Her son's future was at stake. She couldn't afford to think rationally. She would not make excuses for Nick. What he had done was unforgivable.

Dry-eyed, she picked up the phone and methodically punched in numbers. When her sister answered, Stephanie calmly asked Alex to come and get her.

Chapter Fourteen

The wrap-up of his last assignment for the agency took Nick several days. And for the first time in his career he'd resented every agonizing minute. Some ancient survival instinct kept warning him he needed to get back to Stephanie as fast as possible.

There'd been no opportunity to contact her. And logically he'd known she couldn't still be at his place. Yet he'd dialed the house anyway, hoping she'd answer. She hadn't. It was Alex who'd told him Stephanie was at the lab.

Nick got to Stephanie's office late Monday afternoon. She was working at her computer, deep in concentration. For several long moments Nick simply looked at her, almost overcome by the depth of his feelings for this woman. As if sensing his scrutiny, she glanced up at him, and in that instant, his worst fears were confirmed.

She smiled but her eyes didn't warm. There was no welcome in them, none of the passion that had been in them when he'd left her in his bed.

Nick felt as if a vital part of him had been mortally wounded.

"Well, the warrior returns," Stephanie said coolly.

He walked toward her, stopping within three feet of her chair. The coldness seeping into him kept Nick from demanding that she tell him how she'd found out, that she give him a chance to defend himself.

"Were you successful?"

He nodded. "We nailed the scum who were setting up a deal to buy the illegal arms. And the bastards who were supplying them won't be shipping anything. For a while."

Stephanie softened momentarily, knowing how important this assignment had been to Nick. "That's good," she said. "At least we know the world's a little safer now."

"Right," Nick said, his smile was grim. For an insignificant block of time there would be fewer weapons available for use by criminals. But he knew what had been done was an exercise in futility. Another extremist group with the right amount of money would come along, and the dealers would be up and operating again in days. He tried to shrug off the weight of inevitability that pressed in on him.

Once again, Nick thought bleakly, his chosen profession was about to alter his personal life. He'd come full circle. The first time had been in Nam, when he'd been captured and held prisoner. Where months of inhuman treatment and raging infection had started the process that ultimately led to his sterility.

The irony of the situation was that, if not for that gruesome event, he would never have gone to a fertility clinic, would never have fathered Jason. Would never have known Stephanie. And now his job had taken him away at the worst possible moment. And he'd probably lost her.

Nick looked as though he'd been through hell, Stephanie noted. Her heart turned over, but she forced herself to seal off the thought before it could weaken her resolve. She straightened her shoulders. She couldn't afford to feel sympathy for him.

"Tell me something," she began, filling the conversational void. "How did you just happen to be assigned to my laboratory?"

Nick didn't say anything, but the answer was obvious.

"Of course. You set it up," she answered for him. "Very clever. But then I've had the last several days to fully comprehend just how clever you can be."

Nick's face remained expressionless. "Apparently not too clever."

Feeling the need to be on a more equal footing with Nick, Stephanie stood, then turned her back to him. "And how's the investigation here going?"

Nick sighed. "We think we have it solved."

"Good," she said crisply, too agitated to ask for details. She swung around to face him. "How soon can I expect you out of my life?" And Jason's, she added silently, feeling her heart crack. Her son was going to be devastated.

She hadn't told Jason. She'd been too numb with her own pain and sense of betrayal. She'd simply tried to get through one day at a time. Like an automaton, she'd gone through the motions of a normal life. She'd gotten up every morning and gone to work, first praying that she'd hear from Nick, then praying just as fervently that she wouldn't.

Jason had kept asking about Nick, and Stephanie had made up one lie after the other.

"I need to talk to Jason," Nick said quietly.

"You mean your son?" She wrapped her arms around herself. "Go ahead, you can say it."

"Yes," Nick said deliberately, his gaze unwavering. "My son." Her words hurt much deeper than he'd anticipated. Her anger was clear, but it was the carefully concealed anguish that ripped at his heart.

He hadn't denied it, a little voice pointed out unnecessarily, and new anguish assaulted Stephanie. She'd hoped, prayed, that she'd misinterpreted what she'd found in that folder on Nick's desk. "Then I guess you could say that you've successfully wrapped up three missions. Not bad for one day's work."

Fear made Nick strike out verbally. "What the hell are you talking about?"

She began pacing to keep herself from collapsing into a whimpering heap. Holding up one finger, she said, "You stopped an illegal-arms deal." Another finger joined the first, and she started back across the room. "You solved the mystery of who's been breaking into the lab's computer system."

Stephanie stopped suddenly and pinned him with a glittering stare. "Or has this investigation simply been a front?" She waved her hand to cut off any explanation. "And of course," she continued, "your third one, Jason." Her voice cracked on her son's name.

"Stephanie, let me explain," Nick said. It was as close as she'd ever heard him come to pleading.

"Explain what? I've already worked it out for myself. I admit I might be a bit naive, but don't forget, I am a genius," she added with sarcasm. "And it doesn't take one to figure this out."

"And what have you figured out?" His voice was flat, with no emotion left in it.

She answered his question with one of her own. "How are you going to do it?"

Nick raked a hand through his hair. "Do what?"

"Take Jason away from me."

Nick thought he'd hurt before, but nothing compared to the torture of her words slicing into him. He knew he'd destroyed her trust. But could she really believe he'd do something that despicable to her? To Jason? He clenched his jaw against the pain. "I said I wanted to talk to him, not take him away from you."

Stephanie was certain she was coming apart in small, painful pieces. She couldn't deny him the right to see her son. *His* son. "First, I want your promise that you'll let me tell Jason about this in my own time."

Nick slid his hands into his pockets to keep himself from reaching for her, dragging her against him, and kissing her into submission. "And do you plan to tell him?" A heaviness settled in his gut as he realized that his worse fears were coming true. Stephanie wasn't going to allow him to be part of their lives. The two most important people in the world to him were slipping away from him.

The remaining color in Stephanie's face drained away.

"Forget it." Nick sighed heavily. "You have my word. I won't discuss this with Jason."

"All right. Come by the house tonight after eight."

"Thank you," he said rather formally. "Then you and I are going to talk."

"There's nothing left to say," She simply wanted him out of her life. Didn't she?

"Wrong," Nick said ominously. "There's one hell of a lot."

"You used me," she whispered, throwing out her strongest defense. "You used me to get to the most precious person in my life."

"And you used *me.*"

She shook her head, denying the accusation. "How?"

"Without a part of me, Jason wouldn't be here."

"I realize that," she said, frowning in confusion.

Nick strode to the door and opened it. He looked back at Stephanie, sorrow etched in his face. "The sperm that gave us Jason should have been destroyed after my wife's death," he told her flatly. Then he was gone.

She stared at the empty doorway. Oh God, she thought in despair, they'd both been innocent pawns. But she wouldn't let that influence her. Would she?

The doorbell rang promptly at eight, and Stephanie allowed Jason to beat her to it, probably because she wasn't certain she was ready to face what was coming. He eagerly jerked open the door to admit Nick.

He looked as if he'd aged ten years since she'd seen him that afternoon. Lines of fatigue shadowed his face, along with at least a day's growth of beard. He appeared more formidable, more dangerous, than Stephanie could remember.

"Where have you been?" Jason demanded, throwing himself into Nick's arms and hanging on for dear life.

Stephanie watched Nick close his eyes and savor the feel of hugging his son. And she felt a small crack in her resolve.

"Sorry, champ, but I had some things I had to take care of." Nick set Jason away from him. "How're you doing?"

"Fine. But I sure've missed you."

"I've missed you, too," Nick said, looking over at Stephanie.

They were still standing in the entrance hall, she suddenly realized, remembering her manners. "Won't you come in?" she said stiffly, leading the way down the steps to the great room.

Nick followed several paces behind, but she felt his gaze burning into her.

Jason bounded down ahead of them and plopped onto one of the sofas. "I figured you must be mad at me, after all."

Stephanie felt something like grief move through her. Jason loved Nick so much. She carefully chose a chair several feet away, wondering if Nick wanted her here, wondering if he would keep his earlier promise not to tell Jason who he was.

"No, Son," Nick sat down on the sofa beside Jason. "I promise I'll tell you if I'm ever mad at you. Deal?"

Jason grinned in relief. "Deal."

"Son, I need to ask you about something important."

"Okay," the boy said, matching Nick's serious mood. "What?"

Nick propped his elbows on his knees and studied his clasped hands. "You know about what's been happening with the computers at your mom's lab?"

Jason nodded, his expression becoming distinctly uncomfortable.

"I think we know who's been doing it."

"You do?" he asked, his face now guarded. "Who?"

"You." Nick didn't soften the word, but he turned his head to look at his son.

Stunned, Stephanie had to force herself not to speak out. But some instinct told her that it was best to let Nick handle this.

Jason didn't deny it. In fact, he said not a word.

"Why didn't you mention it to anyone when they started investigating?" Nick's tone was gentle, but Stephanie heard the underlying core of steel.

"Nobody asked me," Jason told him with the simple logic that only the very young possess.

"Didn't you think you should offer to tell them?"

"They talked to everyone else, but nobody talked to me. So I figured what I was doing must not matter. I didn't mean to hurt anything," he added earnestly.

"I know you didn't."

"Are you mad at me, Nick? Is that why you haven't come to see me?"

"I told you, I'll let you know when I'm mad at you. You won't have to ask," Nick assured him again. "Now, you want to tell us how you did it?"

Stephanie's question exactly. Jason was a seven-year-old child. How in heaven's name had he cracked the lab's security system? she wondered.

She watched Jason run his fingers through his hair, much as she'd seen Nick do on countless occasions. Like father, like son, she thought, feeling the squeeze of sadness in her chest.

Jason looked sheepish. "Well," he began. "I learned by practicing on the computer in Mom's room." He darted a look at Stephanie. I figured out what the codes were. And then I used 'em sometimes when I went to the lab with Mom."

It made sense. And it explained why the security breaches had been so amateurish and so random, Stephanie thought. She'd created most of the codes for the lab, and she'd done them here on her own computer. All Jason had needed was to break her codes, then access the other programs at the lab when he was there with her. She just hadn't realized how talented, how resourceful, her son could be. Or why.

Nick mulled this bit of information over. "Okay. I understand how you did it. I think," he added to himself, his smile a bit wry. "You want to tell us why?"

Jason squirmed and took a particular interest in a loose thread on his shorts.

When he didn't answer, Nick prompted, "Son, I'd like to know why."

He sighed heavily. "I was trying to figure out a way to find out about my dad. I'm sorry, Mom," he said in a rush, looking at Stephanie. "I wasn't doing anything bad."

The ache in her heart seemed to fill her whole being. "Oh, honey." She went to Jason and sat beside him. As if drawn by a magnet, Stephanie's gaze met, then locked, with Nick's. The silent message in his eyes was so strong, she had to force her attention back to Jason. "You should have asked me if you wanted to know about your dad."

Her son looked miserable, but finally said quietly, "I didn't think you wanted to talk about him."

In that instant Stephanie knew that what was between Nick and her had to be resolved for Jason's sake. And for her own sake, a painful corner of her heart cried. She glanced at Nick, acutely conscious of the leashed tension in him.

She brushed Jason's hair away from his face and gave him a kiss. "We'll talk about this as much as you want tomorrow," she told him. "Go up and get ready for bed."

"Will you come up and tell me a story?" he asked, hugging her tightly.

"Not tonight, honey. Nick and I have to talk. Tell your... tell Nick goodnight."

He gave a sigh of acceptance. "Okay."

Nick pulled his son into a hug. "I'll see you soon."

"It won't be too long, will it?" he asked, his voice muffled by Nick's shoulder.

Nick squeezed his eyes shut before answering. "I promise, if it's going to be a very long time, I'll let you know. Okay?"

"'Kay."

"One more thing, champ."

Jason leaned back so he could look at Nick. "Yeah?"

"You do understand that it isn't right to break into other people's business without their permission. Right?"

Jason nodded his head, looking contrite. "I'm sorry. I won't do it again."

Nick patted him on the shoulder. "That's good, Son."

"'Night, Nick. I love you." Jason started toward the stairs.

"I love you, too." Nick watched until Jason had disappeared up the stairs before bringing his gaze back to Stephanie.

"I had no idea what he was doing." She shook her head. "Thank you. You handled that brilliantly."

Nick shrugged. "No big deal. Sometimes it's easier for a boy to talk to a man."

"He needs you."

In one swift motion, Nick surged to his feet and strode over to the window, staring out into the fall twilight.

"I won't try to stop you from seeing him."

He swung around to face Stephanie, clearly surprised.

"I can't deny you your son anymore than I can deny Jason his father." She had to turn away from the emotion in Nick's glittering eyes.

"Let me see if I understand you correctly. You're willing to let me see Jason anytime I want?"

"Yes."

"Just like that, you're willing to share the most important person in your life with me."

"I'll call my attorneys tomorrow and have them draw up the papers."

"But you're not accepting my offer of marriage?" he clarified.

Stephanie hesitated a painful beat. "No."

Nick studied her. "Then I'm not interested."

Stephanie's gaze rushed to his face, but his features were unreadable. "Of course you want to see Jason. He loves you and you love him."

"I can't argue with that," he said, and started across the room toward her.

She backed up a step. "I don't understand."

"Let's see if I can make it clear. You can count me out. Thanks but no thanks. You can keep your deal."

With each statement, Nick advanced another step closer. And Stephanie kept pace in the opposite direction, until he'd backed her into a wall.

"Finally," Nick muttered when she couldn't retreat any farther. He braced a hand on either side of her head, effectively trapping her, and leaned his body into hers. "I have one more mission," he said huskily, "one you failed to mention earlier this afternoon."

"One more mission?" she echoed, the weight of Nick's body against her making her distinctly breathless.

"You and me," he said quietly, his breath feathering her face. "And we're going to settle it tonight. I love Jason beyond measure. I've made it a long time without knowing my son. And Jason still doesn't know that I'm his father."

"I know." Stephanie searched his face, trying to see beyond his hard features. "I thought that's what you wanted to change."

"I want to know what *you* want."

A fragile hope flared to life again. No one before Nick had ever asked her what she wanted. Now, in the most important decision of her life—and his—he wanted to know her wishes.

"Was it all a lie?" she asked him, her heart pounding. "Did you make love to me, tell me you loved me, ask me to marry you, just so you could have Jason?"

Nick anchored her head with his hands, but he didn't kiss her. Instead he kept his mouth a hairbreadth from hers. "Let me put it this way," he told her, his voice sounding like sandpaper on silk. "If you can't believe that I love you, if you won't marry me, then I don't think I can hang around the edges of your life, even for the sake of my son."

Stephanie wasn't certain she'd heard correctly. "You really do love me?"

"Yes!" he groaned, covering her mouth with his.

It seemed like forever since the last time she'd kissed Nick. And it felt wonderful. She clung to him and opened her mouth so he could get as deep as he wanted. A few minutes later, when they were both half out of their minds and breathless, Nick lifted his head.

"There's still something we haven't settled yet," he said, his eyes smokey with arousal, and something else.

"What?"

"I can't give you more children."

She saw the flash of uncertainty in his eyes, and she wanted to cry. Most of all, she wanted to wipe it away forever. "Of course I'd love to have more—" But Nick placed a finger over her lips, cutting off her words.

"You might find someone else," he reminded her, "someone who could give you children."

Stephanie kissed his fingers and gently removed his hand. "But I don't want anyone else's children. Don't you see? I want kids with the man I love." She pulled his mouth to hers and gave him a long, hard kiss. "That's you. And you've already given me one very beautiful, very precious child. If you can't give me others, then I'm more than content with the one we already have.''

He closed his eyes to contain what her generosity did to him. "Are you saying you're going to marry me and create fantasies with me for the rest of our lives?"

She smiled softly. "That's exactly what I'm saying."

"I don't think there's enough hours left in my lifetime to tell you how much I love you."

Stephanie leaned back and looked up at the man she loved. "And I love you. Let's go upstairs and tell our son that he has a father."

* * * * *

Get Ready to be Swept Away by
Silhouette's Spring Collection

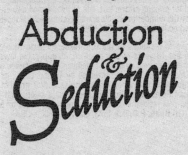

Abduction & Seduction

These passion-filled stories explore both the dangerous
desires of men and the seductive powers of women.
Written by three of our most celebrated authors, they are
sure to capture your hearts.

Diana Palmer
Brings us a spin-off of her Long, Tall Texans series

Joan Johnston
Crafts a beguiling Western romance

Rebecca Brandewyne
New York Times bestselling author
makes a smashing contemporary debut

Available in March at your favorite retail outlet.

MILLION DOLLAR SWEEPSTAKES (III)

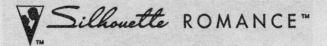

Arriving in April from Silhouette Romance...

Bundles of Joy

Six bouncing babies. Six unforgettable love stories.

Join Silhouette Romance as we present these heartwarming tales
featuring the joy that only a baby can bring!

THE DADDY PROJECT by Suzanne Carey
THE COWBOY, THE BABY AND THE RUNAWAY BRIDE
by Lindsay Longford
LULLABY AND GOODNIGHT by Sandra Steffen
ADAM'S VOW by Karen Rose Smith
BABIES INC. by Pat Montana
HAZARDOUS HUSBAND by Christine Scott

Don't miss out on these BUNDLES OF JOY—only from Silhouette Romance.
Because sometimes, the smallest packages can lead to the biggest surprises!

And be sure to look for additional BUNDLES OF JOY
titles in the months to come.

THE MACKADE BROTHERS

the exciting new series by
New York Times bestselling author

Nora Roberts

The MacKade Brothers—looking for trouble,
and always finding it. Now they're on a collision
course with love. And it all begins with

THE RETURN OF RAFE MACKADE
(Intimate Moments #631, April 1995)

The whole town was buzzing. Rafe MacKade
was back in Antietam, and that meant only one
thing—there was bound to be trouble....

Be on the lookout for the next book in the
series, **THE PRIDE OF JARED MACKADE—**
Silhouette Special Edition's 1000th Book!
It's an extraspecial event not to be missed,
coming your way in December 1995!

THE MACKADE BROTHERS—these sexy, trouble-
loving men will be heading out to you in alter-
nate books from Silhouette Intimate Moments
and Silhouette Special Edition.
Watch out for them!

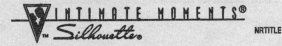

INTIMATE MOMENTS®
™ Silhouette®

NRTITLE

A ROSE AND A WEDDING VOW (SE #944)
by Andrea Edwards

Matt Michaelson returned home to face Liz—his brother's widow...a woman he'd never forgotten. Could falling in love with *this* Michaelson man heal the wounds of Liz's lonely past?

A ROSE AND A WEDDING VOW, SE #944 (3/95), is the next story in this stirring trilogy by Andrea Edwards. THIS TIME, FOREVER—sometimes a love is so strong, nothing can stand in its way, not even time. Look for the last installment, A SECRET AND A BRIDAL PLEDGE, in May 1995.